THE LOVE-ARTIST

THE

LOVE-ARTIST

JANE ALISON

Picador USA
FARRAR, STRAUS AND GIROUX
NEW YORK

www.picadorusa.com

Picador® is a U.S. registered trademark and is used by Farrar, Straus and Giroux under license from Pan Books Limited.

For information on Picador USA Reading Group Guides, as well as ordering, please contact the Trade Marketing department at St. Martin's Press.
Phone: 1-800-221-7945 extension 763
Fax: 212-677-7456
E-mail: trademarketing@stmartins.com

Library of Congress Cataloging-in-Publication Data
Alison, Jane.
  The love-artist: a novel / Jane Alison.—1st Picador USA ed.
    p. cm.
  ISBN 0-312-42006-4
  1. Ovid, 43 B.C.–17 or 18 A.D.—Fiction. 2. Rome—History—Augustus, 30 B.C.–14 A.D.—Fiction. 3. Rome—History—Tiberius, 14–37—Fiction. 4. Black Sea Region—Fiction. 5. Poets, Latin—Fiction. 6. Exiles—Fiction. I. Title.
PS3551.L366 L68 2001
813'.6—dc21   2001055432

First published in the United States by Farrar, Straus and Giroux

First Picador USA Edition: April 2002

10 9 8 7 6 5 4 3 2 1

Two offenses ruined me: a poem and an error.

—Ovid, *Tristia* 2.207

I gave you your life.

Now you're wondering—will I take it, too?

—Ovid, *Medea*, surviving fragment

THE LOVE-ARTIST

PROLOGUE

Now the word is given, the horses are lashed, and the wagon jolts down the dark street, a helmeted soldier seated at each side and Ovid, the exile, between them. Flames glare through the eyes and mouths of stone lanterns, and the blue night air swirls about him like water. The Palatine, crusted with villas, floats off to his left, the Capitoline with its glowing temples to his right; his own house dissolves far behind. His cold hands are clasped together upon his satchel, and he stares, his eyes like the eyes of the lanterns, that word still incomprehensible. *Exile*.

The soldiers came to his house only an hour ago. They stood in the overgrown atrium, in their dazzling armor, and when they told him why they'd come, Ovid—tall and lean, pen in hand—noticed the red wall near his arm gently waver. It was late. "I see," he said, but all he could hear was a humming. "Tomis." He touched the wall with his fingertip to still it. "The Black Sea, you say. *Exile*"—as if in his own voice it might become clear. "But I may bring what I want. My writing things, my books." He watched as his index finger drew a damp line on the wall, from the hoof of a stag to the white teeth of a dog. Then, unaccountably, he felt his mouth stretching into a grotesque hyena grin; he actually heard himself laugh. "Does that mean I can bring *Rome?*"

The soldiers, of course, didn't answer. They placed themselves at either side of the door and waited for him to pack. So Ovid found himself turning slowly, underwater, moving through the red and gold and black walls of his house, his shocked eyes falling upon the familiar bronze, marble, and papery surfaces, with that terrible grin stretching his face, with that terrible word incomprehensible. He stood swaying slightly in his bedroom, on the mosaic skeleton that danced upon the floor. He put some warm clothes, a few tablets, and a stylus in his satchel. Then another pair of shoes, and Carus's book. He stood there, looking around; he knelt and fastened his boots. He walked back into the wet green atrium, past Persilla with her streaming old eyes, past poor Lazar hiding his face in the shadows. "I'm sorry, goodbye," he heard himself say, as if he had been a bad guest. Then he passed for the last time through his own door into the cool spring night, and stepped into the wagon, a soldier on either side.

The blue night swirls by, and there's a dim roar of Rome all around. The wagon has reached the green stretch between the two hills and passes over the cloaca; it threads around the circular temple and, climbing, skirts Marcellus's theater. It would be lit inside now, Ovid realizes. The stage would be glowing saffron red, and there would be the murmur of all the voices, and the intricate hairstyles, and the bare shoulders, and the messages flying, and the swift appreciative glances, and the limb-weakening applause, which has often been for him . . .

The theater drifts by. They reach the river with its marshy spring air, and as the horses break into a gallop Ovid is thrown against one of the soldiers. He's jolted; his heart pounds.

"The thing is," he says—and he's shocked by his voice, how suddenly it flies from his throat—"the thing is, I didn't do anything."

The soldier's gaze shifts his way, and light glances from his helmet, a reflection of the city going by.

"I didn't. I thought Augustus believed me." But Ovid's voice seems to be drifting away. "You see," he says, concentrating with effort, "it was a mistake. I didn't know what Julia was doing. How could I have known?"

The soldier turns. It has nothing to do with him. His instructions were simple: arrest Ovid, remove him from Rome, place him on the ship bound for Tomis, the Black Sea. It's someplace up and over, he vaguely knows, at the edge of the world. A Roman outpost, very cold, always under siege. Uncivilized. Not likely that anyone speaks Latin up there, not even much chance of fresh fruit. What a place for this swan, he thinks, this poet with his tall, gray elegance, his finely arched nose, his feverish look, his leanness. Women were said to rush him on the streets, their dresses flying, bare arms lifted, eyes dilated, delirious to know him . . . *Tomis*.

Ovid has fallen silent, realizing that his words do not matter. The wagon jolts along more slowly, one of thousands rolling through the city, their wooden wheels groaning upon the granite roads. He gazes at the faces passing by—hard faces of fishermen and farmers, their wagons full of octopus, artichokes, and quail, the minor delights of Rome that he won't taste again. A merchant's daughter looks up as she passes, and her mouth falls open in recognition. She covers it with a startled hand.

Now the Aventine is rising to the left, its great black form blocking out the stars, giving off a scent of cypress. They turn onto the Via Ostiensis, swing south. Ovid has become aware of the pain in breathing; he keeps his teeth tightly clenched. They trot by a place that is discreetly marked, but he knows it at once: it's where the Vestals are buried alive when they break their vows to be virgins. Something runs through him, and he finds an arm flying; he finds himself almost laughing.

"He may as well just do that," he cries. "Give me a lamp and food for a day and pack me underground."

The soldier to his left grips Ovid's wild arm. He himself supervised hundreds of suicides some years back, when Augustus was cleaning out the senate, not to mention the swift executions when they didn't go willingly. Exile seems to him rather mild. "It's not the end of the world," he says.

Ovid looks away, sobered. "It is," he says. "I've been there."

Although in his mind he amends himself. He hasn't been there, exactly, not Tomis. Not the western side of the Black Sea, where he is bound now. But the eastern shore he has certainly seen, for that is where he found *her*, Xenia, only a year ago. When he set out blindly on the trip that has ruined him.

Suddenly he feels it streaming behind him, this world that he is leaving. This great city and all that it's made of—the finest things men have created and all the texture of cultured life, books and art and buildings and music, whispers in a marble square, sun shining through an amethyst dress, a glance on the street, sleek onyx statues standing in a row, the flare of recognition in intelligent eyes, the piercing spur of rivalry, the pleasure of praise, the thunder of the crowd as the horses gallop by, a translucent white vase in a garden, walls all figured with myth, the rooms where conversation flies like torches, and everywhere, everywhere, the subtle net of language, whose strands he himself has woven so finely that veils upon veils of meaning have hovered... He is going where there will be nothing: only the silent ground and the hard sky, alone.

The wagon rattles on. He clenches his teeth as the darkened walls roll by, and no one sees or comes.

Where is everyone? Where are the women who were inflamed by his *Loves*—the one who drew him a message in wine on a dinner-party tablecloth, that one who stood before him in an afternoon bedroom, nude? Where are the grand old patricians who clapped him on the back, their eyes wet from the sheer knowing beauty of his *Metamorphoses*? Where are the ox-eyed young men with their groomed dark heads, reading his *Art of Love* for advice? And the old women, keyholes to bedrooms, and the tarty slave girls with their slippery tongues? And the Greek booksellers, who know literature when they see it! Where is Carus? Where are his friends?

All the doors are closed, the shutters drawn for the night, this, his last night in Rome.

Julia?

No, what's he thinking: she's already gone. Augustus's own granddaughter—she had to be gotten rid of. Adultery is the official charge, as Augustus doesn't want known what she's really done. She's been packed off like her mother to a remote island, to live and die, alone. You are a boil, Augustus said. I want you out of my sight.

And *she*, that other, that Xenia? Where exactly is she? She left nothing behind but that jungle in the atrium, a few withered things in the window, and those two chilling lines . . . She even took her door handle.

At the thought of those two lines and all that is lost, a quiver runs through him. "Witch," he whispers. The word flies from his mouth, and his eyes dart up to the night sky with it, as if he expects to see her there, wheeling like the gulls against the lopsided moon. Only blue clouds drift by. She could be anywhere.

In the sea—in the grass—for all he knows, laughing right now in his satchel. He looks down at it sharply, then closes his eyes and passes a damp hand over them.

Palm trees hurry by, and lemon trees, and an illuminated temple. A door to a house opens upon a bright hum of voices and color, and two drunken men come out, laughing. They look up with blurred recognition at Ovid as he is borne by.

Guilt and remorse fan slowly through him, like blood let in a bath. The sickening sense washes up his throat, flows salty into his mouth, but when it reaches his teeth he bites down. No: Xenia did it to herself. She could have given him what he wanted, when he begged her, and he would have undone every-thing—he would have burned the precious thing himself. If she had only told him what she alone was able to *see*, what he so desperately wanted to know.

Whether his work would last. Whether he'd be immortal.

How much could it have cost her to tell?

If only, as Ovid is carried from Rome, the world would draw back its veils and show itself the way Xenia could see it! If only he could see what was to become of him, of his name and his bright, mercurial poems—the palaces and villas that will rise up hundreds of years later all over these famous hills, their ceil-ings and walls made brilliant with frescoes, and the stately gal-leries of paintings, the halls of marble sculptures . . . all glorying *him* and his clever, alchemical stories. If he could see the schol-ars and monks illuminating his verses with tiny images of girls becoming trees, of boys with feathery wings, of cool statues blushing to life. *I'll write about bodies transfigured* . . . He has hoped and begged for this so fervently that his nails have pierced his lean dry palms, as iron nails will pierce other palms only a few years from now; he has forced the blood to pounding behind his eyes with the sheer aching pressure of his ambition; he has, finally, done what he's done, in the terrible force of his desire.

To be *known*. To be *remembered*. To live forever.

Now they've come to the bottom of Rome; they're approaching the Ostian gate. This is it, then. Nothing will stop this steady movement, he's helpless. The wagon keeps rolling forward; the gate rises up with its huge brick arches and all its engraved inscriptions. With a sudden darkness, a smell of damp, the wagon passes under the arch and they're through, out in the stretching fields, the straight road lined with tombs.

Beside him, the soldiers relax. They are out of Rome now. Ovid is gone.

PART ONE

1

It was a very hot day in June when Ovid first saw Xenia, nude and blue, on the farthest coast of the Black Sea, in the corner of the maps where sea monsters coiled and the river Ocean bit its own tail around the world; where he had collapsed upon a fallen tree trunk, his hair thick with salt and his sandals full of needles, exhausted from his journey.

Everyone on board had known who he was, giggling, jostling, pointing him out. By then his *Loves* and *Art of Love* were everywhere—not just in Rome but *everywhere*—the second one especially prized, being so wicked, with instructions on all things erotic, from rendezvous techniques to the most intimate rhythms. Girls murmured his words to each other as they stood before their mirrors; they arranged their hair this way and that and crouched, bare bottomed, looking back alluringly over their rumps. *Oh no, that's not your best view*, they'd whisper to each other, advising as his book tongue-in-cheek coached. *Your side is much better, with your thigh stretched long!* His lines had become veils on the bodies of women as they strolled the streets of Rome, knowing how to deploy that full flank, that flaming nest of hair. He had set the city on fire!

But that, of course, was one of the reasons he'd decided to take this trip east. *The Loves* had barely slipped by, but *The Art of Love* . . . Augustus, intent on reinstating old-time morality in his new empire (after all the blood and proscriptions that had allowed him to establish it), had threatened the book with censorship before it even came out. So in a large dramatic gesture Ovid had burned the text, scattering the ashes upon the Tiber. But of course he had another copy, and, what with the demand created by all the publicity, it was secretly released later. Being rare, the books were exquisitely expensive—and that had come in handy, his funds never being as fluid as those of Augustus's pet poets, who wrote of austere pleasures and of the magnificence of Rome. The emperor's palace had growled at its role in the book's success; Augustus ground his jaw and fixed Ovid with his gray eye from his stone-cold palace on the Palatine. So Ovid had decided, with the advice of Carus and Marcus and the others, that while his latest, *Metamorphoses*, was still at the copyists, he'd just dart off for a time.

But he was glad of it. He was edgy; he was sick of his frivolous reputation: he wanted his image transformed. Vergil, Horace—they were the true poets, gray and grave and weathered, heaven-borne already. But with *Metamorphoses* he thought he'd begun to shed that wearisome slick skin; he'd begun to finger live bones. And now he must continue, deepen—he must start something new. Although he didn't know what yet, which, to tell the truth, was peculiar. Usually by the time he finished one book the next was already pecking, whereas, since completing this latest, he'd felt oddly scraped clean. But with some air, some distance: of course it would come.

It had taken two weeks in that first ship with its magnificent sails to get from Rome to Athens, another two crossing the

Aegean, two again tacking north—that long, even though the winds were favorable, no magpies swooped from the left, no one dreamt of black boars, and the bulls' entrails were always clean. Once they reached Athens, Ovid took a jaunt around the city, had a look at all the ruined statues poking their heads from the fields, remnants of Rome's last sacking. But the weariness of it all irritated him, how handled it had been. All the monuments, artifacts, sightseers, guides. Quackery. Dust. Just seeing it made him dry up inside, made all inspiration expire. He didn't know quite what he wanted—but it must be something more *pristine*, more primeval. So after a week he made the rounds down at the dock and booked passage for Asia Minor. But after a glimpse of Troy he shook his head. Troy, Troy: the very name made him tired, filled his nostrils with old, old dust. The woman, the thief, the great war: the poem. Who could ever compete. He'd always sided with Paris, anyway. Not for his wickedness, though—for his ruin.

At that point Ovid had sent his boy Lazar homeward, wishing to be alone for the rest of his blind adventure. This latest vessel, the one whose railing he gripped now as he stood watching the shadowy green hills go by, had creaked through the Dardanelles, up the Marmara, through the Bosporus, where the water flowed both ways, and had at last broken into the Black Sea.

It was a still twilight, clear and warm, as the ship sailed out of Trapezus and began to curve along the Black Sea's eastern shore, the outermost shore of the world. It sailed past shadowy hills and gorges, sheer black cliffs, pebbled beaches, citrus groves. It moved easily, silent, as the current of this sea flowed counterclockwise; you could just go round and round. Ovid stood on the deck, long fingers gripping the railing, Roman-gray eyes peering into the green hollows and mists. All day he'd had a feeling, the very faintest stirring, that *here*, at the end of the world, he would find what he sought.

It must be something *sharp*, he was thinking. He drummed a finger on the railing and watched a blood-clotted jellyfish pulse through the water. Like a woman's severed head, he noted, like poor Medusa. He thought a moment of the snaky-haired woman, seeing her, singular, fierce, and pitiful, before him. My next subject must be singular, like her, he thought; nothing as promiscuous as those last works have been. *Promiscuous*: he underlined the word in his mind. So many bodies, so many passions. No, he wanted something etched sharp, all alone. A few ideas had been coming to him the farther east he'd sailed, and he'd scratched them quickly into the black wax of his tablets as the ship had pitched and sails had flapped; he'd tucked them safely in his satchel, which he'd sat on henlike throughout the long voyage. Henlike, him! He nearly laughed down at the billowing jellyfish as it disappeared in the wake. Henlike—with his long legs and hawklike nose! But *Ovid* nearly meant "egg," didn't it? An egg with all its perfection and potential, its hint of beginning-and-endness, and the fine surfaces, too, the pale sky of a robin's egg, the porphyry of an ostrich's . . . A surge rushed through him: it had been gathering in him ever since he woke, this hopefulness, this feeling that he was on a trembling edge.

The Black Sea—he looked out in all glinting directions as the sun began to melt behind him. It was famous, and famously double, with a live, fish-swarming surface, but depths that were said to be cold and dead, where absolutely nothing lived and even drowned bodies never corrupted. This region—Pontus, Phasis, the Bosporan Kingdom—was notoriously female and monstrous, and fishy, too, biformed, unreal: you could see it on the maps. Amazons were said to live here, missing a breast but armed. Just beyond the reach of Augustus, the place was ruled by queens; the men were eunuchs; the women ate their own babies. But it was most renowned for the mythical witch Medea. The one who'd chopped up her brother, chopped up a king, chopped up her own children—out of sheer raging jealousy. She'd even burned alive the princess who'd rivaled her. And there was the goddess they worshiped up here, that mermaid with two fish tails for legs, who lured men into caves. Ovid shivered with disgusted pleasure and let a hand hover near his own nether parts, through his blowing linen, as he imagined the position of orifices, the feeling of her scales. But she had wonderful breasts—you saw it in all the bronze things made like her, the doorknobs and mirror handles and so on. Imagine the excitement of passing your hands from those full breasts, down her sides, in at the supple smooth waist, and then swelling out at the hips, feeling the texture change from skin to delicate scale. Was she cold? Or more like a snake, warm and lissome, winding about your legs?

This sea was so clear—there, a bright school of fish! It darted green, turned silver, vanished in the darkness. Of course, the place was best known in greedy Rome for the sturgeon and caviar that were shipped in by the ton. Ovid licked his lips and let the thought of tiny tart eggs pop deliciously in his mouth. He lifted his arched nose to the cool evening breeze. A fantastic place! An inspiring place. He was sure of it.

Up the coast from Ovid's ship, in a stilted house alone in a cove of black pebbles, Xenia was entering her accounts for the week, her glassy hair glowing in the lamplight, her yellow-and-gray eyes intent. *Pharmakal, Magical, Alchemical*: her chart was long and ambitious, with rows of tiny drawings that were codes for secret tasks. This week there'd been one future seen, two babies immunized against murder, a love spell cast, a dream sent, and a litter of spiders cut from an Egyptian sailor's thigh: *that* had been spectacular. It needed a new category, so she drew something small between *Worms* and *Rashes*, although she considered it a little *Exorcism*, too; beside the picture she printed an *x*. That sailor had been horrified, staring down at his blossoming groin. But really, she thought, it was beautiful, all those tiny green legs!

She paused now, pen in hand. And the blue light?

Wings beat in her ribs as she thought of it. To have found that mineral last week, deep in the gloom of the pine woods—a crumbling pale stone, perfectly dull—yet to have seen something in it the way she saw these things, divined. She'd hurried home, powdered it, calcined it, mixed it with egg white, shaped a small bar, and placed it the next day in the sun. And waited. When the sun set, she put the bar in a box and waited again, until it was completely dark, until the waves grew quiet. Then, in the darkness, she opened the box.

Now those wings beat wildly. For when her fingers had tipped up the lid, a miraculous blue glow had flowed into her room. She'd leapt from her chair, exultant—as if she'd created the moon itself! She'd stood there, heart pounding, in that blue glow, wanting to bolt into the world, to *show*. She could streak over the dunes and through the woods to the Phasians—but the Phasians . . . they would only fall silent, as they always did. They'd stand around her in that holy circle, touch their fingers to their brows, lower their cloudy eyes. *It has nothing to do with holiness!* she'd shout—but then that circle, shocked, would shuffle away, and there she'd be, alone.

So she'd simply stood there, in the plain room, gazing at her sliver of moon, until the light had faded.

Outside, the waves were breaking on the pebbles; the pebbles gently clattered; the flame of her oil lamp bent with her breath. Xenia looked at her chart and rolled her pen slowly back and forth over it. That blue light may have faded, but that she had drawn it at all from dull rock: as miraculous as the brilliance of a peacock emerging from a white egg. For to extract light hidden in stone was close, so close, to extracting *life*. Yes, she drew near . . . *Manipulate nature, find the essence of life!*— the alchemical axiom blazed across her chart. Already she could undo almost any sickness, turn black antimony into silver, transform a sullen boy into a lover. She knew what tricks lay in the tissues of plants, what colors were hidden in metals— sleepiness in hellebore, the craving for love in henbane, blue in iron, bright yellow in lead, vermilion in mercury. And somewhere—finer than earth, water, air, and fire, yet hovering inside all four, perhaps in color or light itself—was the *quinta essentia*, the substance of life.

To find the quintessence, to conquer death. Xenia shut her eyes and imagined again what she always imagined: how she would do it—and then how sought after she'd be! How her celebrity would rise billowing like a saffron veil from her shoulders and fly across the seas until she was known clear to the Pillars of Heracles—and how she would be *sung*.

Outside, the waves were gently breaking, rolling in forever. She looked through the rings around the flame, into the stretching darkness. All that sea, all that heavy earth, all that gassy air. She felt at once foolish and small. Of course, she would never find the quintessence. Furthermore, no one would ever know about anything she'd done or all the extraordinary things she could do. She was at the end of the world and would die here, melt back into the elements she imagined ruling. She looked at her chart, her preposterous chart, and rolled it up, tying around it the ribbon she had once dyed with sea purple, extremely hard to extract.

Her room was quiet. The oil flame glowed. The waves sighed as they fell upon the pebbles, and the pebbles clattered. Xenia sat still and counted the beats in her ribs until she couldn't stand it. She was twenty, and although she'd seen the futures of all eighty-nine Phasians, she'd seen nothing of her own but darkness, and suspected that meant she'd die young. She held her hands over the flame, her fingers glowing red, shut her eyes tightly, and then looked up—at the moon, and the Bears, and the Virgin, and Venus. Spring Venus, so clear and brilliant, melting away the silver moon. Venus, whose name was alchemical for copper; Venus, whose name meant love.

Venus made me her subtle love-artist . . .

The words whispered themselves in Xenia's mind, and her fingers crept to the scrolls of poems beside her chart, the scrolls that were nearly as magical as her own.

The poems had rushed among the Phasians from mouth to ear in memorized snatches ever since the fabulous books had been traded to someone this spring by a Greek sailor for a few bags of salt. Books sailed all the way from Rome, books by Rome's most famous, most fashionable poet—the Phasians had been dazzled, beholding the crimson slipcovers and black edges and gleaming bosses. For they'd heard of Ovid from the merchants and sailors who came their way, his image like a god, or even Caesar. They'd been dazzled by the sheer sight of the books and then, when Xenia had deciphered the Latin, shocked. At last they'd been transformed, a new consciousness like light falling upon them, their clothes worn differently, several des-

perate efforts made to control their snaky hair. Within weeks
there wasn't a Phasian girl who hadn't crouched over a pool of
water and turned herself this way and that with newly quizzical
eyes. *Goat girls*, Ovid would call them. *Don't be a goat girl from
the Caucasus—be sure to shave your legs!* Xenia had engraved
that, burning, in her mind, when she'd pored over the books in
private. For in the end the Phasians had given them to her, as
she was the only one who could read, let alone read Latin.

Now she saw again the tantalizing world they conjured illumined in the dark: a woman with complex hair creeping like a
cat through the purple night, a man climbing in a bedroom
window, a sly message written with a jeweled finger in wine, a
brilliant stage strewn with saffron—and that beautiful Corinna,
her clothes fallen away, teasing in shuttered light . . . The sheer
intoxication of that subtle society, of art, of intricacy, of *Rome*.
But, above all, Ovid. She saw him again, as she always envisioned
him, with a wry face, clever long hands, what she half imagined
as leathery wings. He flew in windows, and dryly laughed, and
fled again, mercurial. So brilliant, so urbane—but within his
words was something achingly earnest, something that pierced
Xenia's heart: *Oh god, don't let my name, my work, sink into
oblivious waters . . .*

*Because why write poems if they're not read? It's like dancing
in the dark.*

It was. She shut her eyes and there opened inside her, like
the voluptuous petals of a poppy, the excruciating sense that
between her and this poet was a secret kinship, and a terrible
desire that he *see* her and know: like Amor spying Psyche from
the heavens, and sending down a breeze to carry her off.

Outside, the waves gently broke upon the pebbles, and the
pebbles clattered. Slowly Xenia returned to her plain room, to

herself, to her heart beating in her ribs. She looked down at the
scroll, at Ovid's words written so far away, and after a moment
noted that a few eyelashes had fallen; she dabbed them up and
dropped them into her pink fish-leather bag. She rolled up the
scroll, slipped over it the crimson cover, and tied around it the
silky gold cord. She combed her hair carefully, as she always did
now at night, gathered the strands, tucked them into her bag,
and knotted it. For a moment she held both hands to the lamp
and turned them slowly around. Sure that they were clean,
unhurt, she took her bronze mirror, stepped out of her dress,
and looked carefully at the rest of her body. Unmarked. She
blew out the lamp and got into bed with the pink bag.

In the darkness she nudged the bag close, so that those stray
elements of herself could not wander again at night—if that
was what had happened. Part of herself had slipped out, it
seemed, or something else had slipped in. She still did not
understand it, but she'd had to use a shell that terrible morning
two weeks ago to scrape the blood from her nails. Although
there hadn't been a scratch or a bite on her body, nothing sticky
between her legs—just blood on her fingers, and a few red
smears on her sheets.

With the bag pressed to her stomach, she began to drift. In
the moonlight her skin was so white it shaded to a milky blue,
her hair a glassy halo. Outside, the breeze lifted, speeding ships
over the seas. The Caucasus pines swayed like mourning
women, their scent mixing with that of the seaweed floating on
the waters that rose and fell. Xenia's fingers relaxed upon the
bag, her mouth opening slightly. Her brow furrowed, her
breath quickened, for she had fallen into the dream from which
she always woke shivering. Again it was black and windy, and
she was small, her face at her mother's damp neck. The basket

bobbed on the water, cold at her legs as she was lowered in. Her mother looked at her with hollow eyes, her mouth so dark and red. She nearly smiled, but didn't quite, and put a trembling hand to Xenia's cheek—but then Xenia felt again a shocking surge, and her throat constricted in her screams as she went floating out alone upon the sea.

As Ovid tossed in his tent and Xenia drifted, far away, back around the coast of the Black Sea, through the Dardanelles, across the Aegean, and up on the Palatine in Rome, Augustus's granddaughter Julia lay waiting in her lion-legged bed for her husband, her contempt concealed by the dark. Her urine had been sniffed by the old nurse each morning this week, and today had been decreed the day. So her legs and underarms had been smeared with black wax, and the hairs had been pulled out, through all of which she'd held her face in a smile—the one that had served her each month for a year now, behind which nothing could be seen. There had been the baths, warm, hot, cold, warm, all those efforts to arouse and melt her; then the massages with scented oil, the slaves' hands running up her stripped calves; then he, too, the husband, Aemilius, had been given a bottle of oil, with whispers of how to apply it: all of this stipulated by the official physician, so probing with his bronze speculum, so enthused by the inner topography of the emperor's granddaughter. Had he really never seen the damage?

Julia smiled now, in the dark, feeling her teeth shine like a dog's—she smiled despite the oil's cloying smell, despite Aemilius's rough fingers, whose prints she imagined impressing her smooth inner skin like brands. Had there ever been, she wondered, a female zone more hostile. But *female zone* was an

ancient term, all embroidered with Aphrodite. She wouldn't
use it, then. *Vagina.* Meaning sword sheath. She thought the
word hard, in her mouth.

Now, leaning over her heavily, Aemilius put aside the oil,
the bottle clattering on the floor; he must have imagined he'd
properly prepared her. And with no further ado—the stabbing.
As if someone could possibly like this! Julia winced and concealed her wince at once in a lascivious moan. His monstrous
face, rearing above her in the dark, she regarded through her
lashes. His eyes were shut, mouth hanging open, and his soft
belly began to beat upon her, as did, somewhere, his testicles.
She could not imagine why he had been chosen. Obedience,
blood, she supposed. He looked down at her, eyes black and
drunk; she swooned in response. Then he shut his eyes again,
and she shut hers, too, as the stabbing became—oh, it was
sharp.

God! she thought, trying to tighten herself against it, to conceal that she did. *God, Mother! Why did you leave this to me?*
Oh, but unfair to think this, she knew. Her eyes stung; everything stung; she dug her nails into the mattress and bid herself
think herself away. Her mother had been exiled by Augustus
for her alleged adulteries ten years ago, when Julia herself had
been only thirteen, just beginning to bleed, not knowing yet
where her own blood would take her. *Oh my mother*, she
thought, as again Aemilius ran her through: *you did as you were
told! And with three husbands, too, for you were married off
again and again. Augustus wanted boys, having been so disap-
pointed by you, his only child. And you bore them!*

Julia could see her brothers now in the flashing darkness
behind her lids: young boys with narrow, olive-skinned faces,
their eyes nervous beneath the imperial fringes. They had been

managing, they had been growing, but then the eldest had so strangely died at just the age he might assume power, and the second—how odd—he'd died, too. The third had been exiled last year, shipped off for an unspecified crime. *So, Mother, all your boys put out of the way. Could it be because Augustus dismissed his first wife when she bore only you, and married Livia that very same day, and this new empress came pregnant already?*

So why am I being bred, too! When Livia's son is waiting! But she knew why, of course: she was Augustus's blood; her loins were the most valuable.

Her loins: now, in the dark, Julia nearly laughed aloud. These precious loins and all that was in them she would rip out with her own hand rather than let them bear fruit for Augustus.

At last Aemilius was finishing. The final stab came, so violent that she felt herself rip and could not restrain her cry but cloaked it quickly in something sounding like pleasure. Then the final shudder, and he fell upon her, his mouth open at her ear. The smell of him, of his wetness mingling with her own, the fishiness, the stench of cut onions, of blood.

"This time for certain," he gasped in her ear.

And she gasped back, "Yes."

2

The air was full of steam the next morning, when Ovid's ship glided up the coast to Xenia's pebbled cove. Steam hung among the pine trees, among the vines with their yellow bell flowers, among the tangerines, oleanders, azaleas, and persimmons. Everything green was crawling, unfurling monstrously large leaves. The buzzing of bees was dense; the black pebbles themselves seemed to crack.

Xenia floated in her pool in the woods, troubled. Despite the bag, despite the sweating heat, she had been shivering when she woke this morning, and there had been mud on her knees. Inexplicable, mud. So was something slipping in—was she herself slipping out? The air was so full, so unstable, so *treacherous*. She decided to bind her mouth at night. Gripping water grass, she held her breath and pulled herself down to the rock.

Underwater, Xenia didn't notice a ship slowly gliding along the shore. She didn't see how a tall figure stood at the prow, with a lean greyhound head and long fingers; or how, once the ship anchored, he lurched as he stepped into the smaller boat that would row him closer in and barked out a brief, excited laugh, setting his Roman nose to the breeze. For he had seen cattle standing knee-deep, grazing upon the seaweed. Cattle in the sea! Then perhaps he'd see dolphins swim through the trees . . . The place was fantastic: he'd known it. The sea breeze billowed through him as if he were a sail, and his imagination went skittering.

From underwater, up in her pool, of course Xenia saw none of this. She certainly did not see Ovid's long brown fingers, patterned with a tracery of salt, tightening upon his satchel as he stepped from the small boat and onto the black pebbles. She might almost have heard the pebbles grate and squeak beneath him, though, the sound traveling from the sea, along the stream, up to her pool in the woods.

Ovid heard it and glanced down at the polished black eggs upon which he found himself standing. His first contact with this weird, remote shore: he underlined it in his mind. *Black eggs*. Up the beach, fish were being gutted for their eggs and smoked; he could see the soft trails wafting into the air. And just now two girls walked along the beach, holding a basket of jumbled, feather-flecked eggs between them. Orbs of porphyry, he said to himself, imagining the polished surface beneath his forefinger and quick thumb. Seagull eggs, of course. He smiled at the staring girls, delighted, proprietary. Seagull eggs, egglike pebbles, fish with their precious egg sacks: at once he stitched it all together with his name. And so felt himself welcomed, given full license in this quite remote, quite un*real* region.

He trod swiftly over the pebble beach, noting how like mosaic it was, a surface made of bits, although cruder, more pristine. *Pristine!* Again pleasure flared through him. It was what he had been after: a primeval place, antediluvian.

Xenia, meanwhile, had sunk once more. She could hold her

breath for a very long time and often practiced, in case of an exorcism. She kicked, disturbing a crab, and sank deeper. Otherwise she might have heard those Roman sandals and their weighty burden crunching over the beach, pausing as he glanced with curiosity at her little house, then climbing over the bright dunes, lunging through the pines, sinking into the sand and the needles, stopping to shake out a few grains. She might have sensed the way the lanky figure shoved away boughs of rhododendron as he staggered through the woods. She might have known how at last he slashed a wet lean wrist across a wet brow, dropped his heavy satchel beside him, collapsed upon a mossy fallen trunk just paces away, and struggled from his heavy linen, from his ruined sandals, as his eyes and hot throat impatiently hurled themselves toward her glassy pool.

Out of breath at last, she pressed her palms upon the rock and, with a final flourish of bubbles, pushed herself up, crashing into air. The cool water fell away from her bluish body and she banged her ears, kicked one leg and then the other free of drops and grassy strands, shook herself in a wild spasm, and squatted for her clothing. Lingering a moment, she placed her palm upon the pool's surface, as lightly as a water strider, and pondered her reflection. Then she stood and, poking one arm through the sleeve of her dress, saw for the first time with a force like a blow the pair of shocked Roman-gray eyes among the vines. She hurried away into the greenery.

3

Remarkable. The fine point of Ovid's stylus scratched at the black wax on his wooden tablet, which he'd placed near, but not too near, the oil lamp by the window. He was in the small stilted house he'd rented up the coast a distance from that pool, by the river, once he'd made his way through the woods and found the Phasians. A house, an old woman to bring him meals, someone first to gather the things he'd left upon the beach.

A halo of insects hovered around the flame—river-born, almost transparent insects he'd never seen before; they must be native to this warm, freakish land. Now and then one plunged in, flared briefly, fell upon his tablet, and was flicked away by an impatient finger. It was so humid that his wrist sweated and stuck to the wax. He shook it and was absurdly startled by the clatter the tablet made as it fell to the table. He resumed.

Remarkable! He would have liked to write it again, even, for further emphasis, but didn't have the room and knew better, although he did allow himself artless indulgences in wax that would be unthinkable in the finished stage of papyrus. He underlined the word instead—*Mirabile!*—with a long, decisive scratch. A flurry of names followed: *Salmacis, Hermaphroditus, Arethusa, Narcissus*; the last one he underlined twice. For that girl by the pool somehow made *flesh* the figures he'd dreamt up, the ones who filled his latest work, his marvelous *Metamorphoses*. Unreal figures, part fantasy, part myth, flitting through transformations: girls who, running, become water or trees, boys who dissolve into their reflections. She had simply risen from that pool, her skin its watery color, exactly as he'd have written it. Ovid laughed out loud at the conceit, with that dry bark he had. *Absurdus*, he printed large.

Now, at any rate, he could actually see the places his imagined figures inhabited; he could smell that heavy, moist, narcotic air, infused with those sweet white flowers. So there really were places—ringed pools, secret groves—where anything could happen. Where human rules could be broken, where laws of nature could be stretched, where the edges of bodily things might dissolve . . .

His *Metamorphoses*. The copyists would be done with it in another month, and then—it would be out. He was glad not to be in Rome, waiting. He had high hopes for this one, the highest. It *must* please Augustus; Ovid praised him in it, twice. It must make him forget that erotic stuff, while Ovid was not in Rome to provoke him. Let him read this new thing, and soften.

Again he saw the perspiration upon the brows of Marcus and Julius that night in his red-walled dining room, when they'd warned him that Augustus's displeasure might have serious consequences someday. How preposterous, he'd replied loudly—he was just a *poet*, it would never come to that! Hadn't Augustus himself chosen Ovid way back when, selected him from among the other boys in his sleepy village to come to

Rome, study law, and be turned into a proper patrician? Hadn't
Augustus given him a horse? To which Marcus replied that,
horse or not, Ovid hadn't in fact become a *proper* anything,
least of all the stately lawyer Augustus had banked on. Ovid
laughed, too explosively, swinging his long arms as he paced
and explained what his friends well knew: that he'd tried very
hard but had been a terrible lawyer—Augustus would be the
first to admit it; that he just did not have patrician blood; that
he'd never been anything at heart but a poet.

But there were poets and *poets*, Marcus retorted. *Serious* ones
who weren't out to undermine the empire. Again Ovid laughed,
outraged, astonished. He had never been out to undermine anything! Augustus's moral empire least of all, with its banning of
adultery, abortion, sorcery, and so on; nothing had been further
from his mind! A few of the poems, admittedly, went too far . . .
but hadn't he been sorry? Hadn't he burned them himself?
Even though, as had been well established (here he produced
the citation), the book explicitly warned virtuous women to stay
away, so how could it possibly corrupt them? At any rate: no, he
had no interest in politics—surely his slinking out of law school
had proved that. It was only *life* he wanted to pin down, only
shocked living bones he wanted to touch, probing deep in
human flesh. And hadn't he finally begun to do this—with his
brilliant, penetrating *Metamorphoses*? Augustus himself would
be moved when he read it! So Ovid had declared, full of bluster,
his face shining and hot. But he'd seen the look in his friends'
eyes and felt his own anxiety, so had agreed to absent himself
for a while.

He domed the oil flame with his hand and pondered his
glowing red bones. He looked out at the sky, at the dark shifty
depths, and had an acute sense of himself as a man, on earth,

gazing up. Human, divine: like his own winged Daedalus, how he longed to soar between. Again that agonizing desire rose hot and urgent in his soul.

To be *known*. To be *remembered*. To live forever.

He saw himself now as he'd been just six weeks ago, when he set out from Rome. Standing on the deck of that sea-nymph ship, with her gold and red and white sails, carved bust at the prow, fish tail at the stern, he'd squinted out at the crowd of women fluttering their veils at him on the dock. As the ropes were loosened and the ship bucked, he flung up his arm in a wave and laughed, drawing wild circles in the sky, imprinting his initial there as he so painfully wanted to. But, at that very moment, with the sails snapping, the gulls shrieking, the water splashing upon the nymph's heaving sides, he was shocked to find his throat suddenly thick, his eyes stinging. It was a fore-boding, he knew it at once. Not the sort that would prevent the ship from sailing—nothing like a crow cawing, or a dream of a goring black bull, which of course meant shipwreck—but per-sonal: a stabbing sense of loss to come. The veil of light and color around him was abruptly pulled away, and for a fleeting moment the world was stark, mineral, reduced. The wind stole his gasping breath, and the sea frothed and sloshed at the ship's flanks, churning gray and deep. He had felt at once distinctly smaller, and cold.

Ovid shivered now; the oil flame flickered; he rubbed the alarmed hairs on his arms. "*Absurdus*," he whispered, and took comfort from the sound of his voice.

Somewhere before him in the dark was the sea, with its con-stant breathing, so slight as to be forgotten until he made an effort to notice it again, and then it was insistent. His satchel lay by his foot, and the blank tablets and scrolls were arrayed

before him on the table. He took a breath, compelling himself
to accept this green, heavy air, nothing at all like Rome's dry
dust. He put down his stylus, cracked his knuckles, rubbed his
lips, and pondered.

This rough wood table, this rough wood floor, this peculiar
hut with its wobbly legs plunging into a grassy hillock, the
river gurgling all around. The Phasians lived behind him, in
their village of houses just like this, with their pine-log boats,
the smell everywhere of smoked sturgeon, watchful women in
the doorways weaving linen. These people had been famous
once for their gold and slaves and fabulous witch; now they
dealt only in fish, timber, and cloth, here beyond the edge of the
empire, awaiting the merchants who made the long trip. They
drew their maps on wood, he'd seen—everything about them
was wooden: their houses, their boats, even their armor. Their
skin, too, he thought, and their hair ... He'd like to see their
toes. Like people growing back into the forest. They spoke a
sluggish pig Greek, but they said there was one among them
who knew Latin and, they hinted, other things besides.

That girl, he thought, or whatever she was.

Crashing from the water like that! A perfectly still pool of
water! He'd nearly swallowed his own tongue. Who knew what
sort of place he'd landed in? Fishy, monstrous, unreal.

Amazons, for instance. He absolutely believed in them. War-
rior women, their strong sweating thighs clutching galloping
horses, wild howls coming from their parched, cracked mouths.
He'd like to see one. He'd certainly like to see the place where
the childish breast had been seared away. Imagine the sound of
that being done! Would there still be a nipple? A ghost of a nipple, a hollow? Or just a sheet of glossy, numb skin? And not just
Amazons: witches, eunuchs. Women who ate their own babies.

But back to this girl.

He thought of her body, with its bluish marbled skin and that streaming, glassy hair. Did she live there, in that pool? He'd been stunned by a swift impression of mottled ice, before she'd shaken and stamped and gathered her things and abruptly marched away. Her flesh had seemed so youthful and dense, deliciously full! Nothing at all the way his own aging olive skin would look after a spell in cold water. But gelid, the blue veins visible beneath the clear skin, like living water beneath ice.

Ice. It was so very warm here. Ovid drew his damp wrist across his damp brow. He shut his eyes in the wet heat, imagining so strongly he nearly *felt* the girl's skin melting at the touch of his tongue. For it wasn't just her appearance, he finally had to admit. The moment those wild eyes had flown at his, he had felt it again, utterly plumbed, and he wondered now if it was happening once more, how often in one life it could happen.

The news of Ovid's presence had run like the river itself all around the Phasians' stilted houses. Rome's most famous, most fashionable poet was holidaying among them, of all people! When he could have been in Baiae or Surrentum or any luxury spot in the world! The news ran round and round, glinting on the surface of the moonlit brackish water; and when it had circled every house—so that Phasian boys drew oiled hands through their hair in efforts to be sleek Romans, so that Phasian girls and women stared in thrilled horror at each other and howled the disappointment of their plain dresses and lack of art—the news traveled then, more slowly, like a nighttime eel, along the slender branch of the river that flowed from the Phasians and coursed through the woods until it broke into the cove where Xenia lived, alone.

All afternoon she had gone over it, trying to see again what she thought she'd so fleetingly seen, *whom*, hidden in the bushes—as if drawn there by her will. Now the miraculous confirmation reached her with a violence that blasted her body like Semele receiving Jove undiluted, and she stood paralyzed, her fate rushing about her ears.

4

Just after dawn, Ovid found himself creeping through the pine woods. The air was fresh, tinged with the scent of rhododendron and narcissus. Pale light streamed sideways through the prehistoric trees; a morning mist rose from the floor of needles and sand and hovered among the vines. What is it that makes the prehistoric—the *pristine*—seem not old but new? he wondered.

Twigs snapped; dewy bushes shuddered; he could hear his own gasping, nervous breaths. He told himself with irritation that he must learn to be more pantherish. The columned and stone-slabbed streets of Rome had not taught him to slink through woods; he must remember his boyhood days, dodging boars among the chestnut woods of Sulmo. Now he was so tall: the boughs scraped his face; he had to duck and swing at the foliage, swipe constantly at whirring mosquitoes. On he plunged through the pines until the fallen needles grew sparser, the damp sand softer and deeper, and at last he broke out of the woods, into the fresh beach morning. There, in sight of the breaking waves and her little house, he crouched behind a clump of shrubs growing on a low dune.

He presumed it was her house, anyway—if she lived in one at all, and not in water itself. He hadn't seen her again, although he had been among the Phasians for several days, buying porphyry eggs and smoked sturgeon and the odd pheasant. She couldn't possibly be one of them, with their thick black brows and staring black eyes—eyes the color of the seaweed floating out there now, where an inexplicable cow grazed, its tail swishing at the surf as it rose.

He was near enough to the house to see the stone table outside and various withered things dangling from the eaves. A weathered basket hung there, too, and a ladder rose from the pebbles to the door. There were a few small windows, one facing the sea, with what looked like glass objects on the sill. He settled behind a beach rose, poked his long fingers into the smooth, crusted sand, and squinted through the bush in the still morning air, the sun now clear above the hills.

After a while, when his eyes had begun to wander, her door suddenly swung open. He crouched lower, and the girl appeared—or he thought it was she; he could hardly believe it. Her pale hair was no longer glassy but wild, her face distorted. She stared at her hands as if they were spiders, held out before her, fingers splayed. She clambered down the ladder and ran across the beach, and as she flew past him he saw that her fingers were bloody.

Leaning forward, he peered through the leaves. She was squatting in the water, plunging her hands in again and again and shaking them violently, as if to fling them away. At last she held them up before her. They didn't appear to be hurt. But she wasn't yet done—for now she doubled over and slapped at her feet, her ankles, her shins, as though to make sure she was there.

Ovid's nose twitched at the touch of a rose, and he became horribly aware of a yellow tuft of pollen. He controlled his quivering nostrils and managed not to sneeze—but somehow had she heard him? All the way from the water? For she spun around, fixed a dire stare in his direction, then coiled and sprang, flinging herself into the sea. Her greenish body hung inside a wave.

He remained behind the shrub, his forgotten fingers stuck deep in the sand, watching her form glimmer in the water. *Glaucus*, he thought, without trying. *Galatea*. Precisely how he envisioned his creatures, his wild, ambiguous beings. It was uncanny the way she embodied them. He almost thought she'd transform before his eyes: turn into water itself, sprout a tail.

But those hands.

He sat up. Surely there was something in the house, some prosaic explanation? She must have *done* something.

Then why so startled, so horrified? As if she woke to find them lying there, on the pillow beside her cheek! He shivered with cold delight.

The rolling surface of the sea glinted as the sun rose. Ovid squinted, searching the swells for her form, but she had swum deep, or was gliding behind a wave, or was over there hidden by rocks. He had a sudden urge to get up and run to her house and climb the ladder and see what was in there—or, better, to hurl himself into the water and grip that slippery, slender, protean form and make her say what she'd done.

A sudden breeze swept in, napping the surface of the sea; it hurried over the pebbles and damp sand toward him on the dune, bearing with it a cool, mineral scent, chilling. The petals of the beach rose trembled at his unshaved cheek. From the house, from the front door, came a clamorous rattle.

He looked about, furtive, unpleasantly aware of what he was doing. He rose on his cracking knees and hurried away through the pines, leaving a scrap of linen on a spiteful thorn.

Moments later Xenia stood dripping where Ovid had been, the roaring in her ears drowning out the sea. She'd almost been blinded by what she'd seen: not just the man himself, lean, slouching, elegant, *famed*, but so much behind him, fluttering about him, all those tiny figures! A winged boy, one with a fish tail, a boy-girl, a weeping tree . . . It was dizzying; she'd never seen such richness, such *life*—colors as brilliant as a peacock! And that he'd crouched there with his famous, interested eyes, those eyes fixed upon *her* . . . The very thought was undoing, and she dropped to the ground—but there were his footprints, flown to her from Rome. She trembled. Then she saw the scrap of cloth left behind and plucked it from the thorn—a token! Looking down again, she discovered the holes made by his fingers. He hadn't just watched her—he'd been rooted, *enthralled*.

She slipped a finger into a hole, and a flush ran over her cheeks. Was it still warm? Pulling her hand away, she looked at it, only then remembering the blood. But the troubling thought flitted by, for her mind was racing like the wind. He'd come to her—but how long might he stay? And then what? She panicked. She must cut her finger and a lock of her hair; she must use this scrap of cloth, and these holes in the sand, and the crimson-covered book itself: yes, she'd even have to burn his poems. She ran from the dune to her house, love spells flying from her tongue.

5

During the following days, Ovid spent hours staring at his stack of blank tablets, at the sea, at the sun as it sank, at the gassy blue rings around his oil flame at night. Often his hand rose above a tablet, stylus sharp and ready, but just as often it faltered and fell. More than two months had passed, he realized, since he'd left Rome, more than two months since he'd written a real word. The black wax of his tablets was as mute as the sea, and he began to have an empty spiraling feeling, as if inside him were the bare whorls of a shell. So he felt entitled to observe her again.

Since the morning at the beach he'd seen her twice. First by chance, in the village. She stood out so with that webby whirl of hair and white skin among all the wooden Phasians; her arms were full of wreaths of some sort, amulets, little packets. For she was a pharmaka; the woman who brought Ovid his cucumbers and pheasant had told him. Something of a magus, an alchemist, too. "You mean a witch?" he'd asked, but the woman had dropped her eyes, preferring to use her own words.

He could not believe he hadn't seen it at once. The withered things hanging from the eaves, all those glass devices on her sill . . . But, of course he'd never actually seen a witch before. Although a few were rumored still to exist, somewhere, despite Augustus, in Rome.

The Phasians had told him: like others of her kind, Xenia's ears or eyes were differently configured, so she could hear and see the tiny particles that flew from people—their thoughts, dreams, curses, and glimpses of their futures. It had become clear when she was six and began screaming and sobbing, slapping at her face. The Phasians, with whom she lived at the time, had been only a little surprised. They'd watched her, silent, in a circle, their index fingers to their brows. For they'd always suspected, ever since finding her in that sodden basket on the beach, a blue, shuddering child with terrible, betrayed eyes.

"Exposed, was she?" Ovid broke in. "By her parents?" The Phasians looked at him as if to say that she couldn't possibly have had parents; it was the sea that had spawned her. Yet they'd taken her in and raised her, and when she'd confirmed their suspicions with those screams and visions they'd simply tied her up and given her for four years each to a magus, an alchemist, and a pharmaka, so that her wild skills could be disciplined. After her training Xenia had returned to them, laden with scrolls and devices, slim and controlled and proud, but still with those terrible eyes. The Phasians built her a house in the cove she'd washed up in—

"Alone?" They looked at him: of course. They kept to their side of the woods, going to her only when they needed to. She cured their rashes and made love charms—

"That work?" Oh yes, they nodded. Once she'd done a *defixion*—burned the hair and the token and said all the magic words—you were fixed, nothing to be done. And she'd tell you, too, if you wanted, your future.

"Your future, really?" asked Ovid, his forgotten fingers stroking quickly at his knee. No doubt about it, they said; she could even point out your grave.

She'd been pale and haughty among the villagers when Ovid saw her there; they grew silent and moved away as she approached. But when she caught sight of Ovid, he saw with delight a tremor run through her, the minute faltering of the footstep that he was so adept at perceiving. She knew who he was, it seemed. They'd said she knew Latin; she might even have read him. She gathered herself at once, kept gliding forward, her eyes far off, uninterested. As she came close enough for him to note the intriguing blue shadows around the neck and sleeves of her dress, she slowly drew her eyes from their distant spot and let them light upon his—just a single breathless moment—before she coolly dropped him and moved on. He was startled: not just by those eyes seen close, one sea gray, one nearly golden, but by the violence with which he felt that look. He turned away, embarrassed, shaken. How many times could this happen? With his Corinna, the woman the world knew from his *Loves* as Corinna, it had been just like this: all at once, obligatory, nothing to be done. Yet the glance had seemed so measured, so artful . . . Yes. *The Art of Love*, book three. She *plotted*!

So he felt entitled, and two nights ago he went out. Over the grasses he strode, through the nettles and into the forest of Caucasus pines. Wouldn't everyone in Rome delight to see you now, he thought, buffooning the part you perfected in *The Loves*— sneaking in shadows, stumbling over the odd shrub, hands stretched before you, perspiring, lit up occasionally by the entertained moon, all in quest of a girl. The motif? The lover's nighttime vigil, the lover begging on his girl's doorstep, hoping for that slim piece of luck, that slim bar of light parting the door from its frame.

It had started this way with Corinna, late-night creeping, and ended this way, too—all that agony, so many years ago. In invisible stages he was reduced from lover to adored husband— that's what her silent eyes had said—to irritant, to besieger. *You're like a crow!* she screamed on the day that was the beginning of the end. *Stop watching!* He could still hear the tearing edge of her voice, still see her beautiful bare back as she walked angrily away. But he didn't stop, did he, and at last she fled the hungering monster he'd become. He didn't even see his transformation until it was complete, until he heard his own hoarse voice on her dark street, saw his own thieving hand pounding on her door, the hand she'd so often pressed to her hot, troubled eyes. All he could do then was kill the whole thing, through the promiscuous rampage he'd called *The Art of Love.*

So damp, the air, it smothered; it pressed against his tense temples. Ovid waited until he could breathe again, then shook his head hard, lifted his shoulders, and plunged on, leaving the ghostly Corinna behind him. He had been very young. So had she.

At last he heard the sea, those weak little explosions of water; breaking out of the woods, he saw the vast blackness glinting under the sky. And there was the girl's house, the moon at that moment sweeping back the clouds and illuminating it, stark and solitary on its pebbled landscape. He would climb the ladder and, holding tight, swing his body over to the window that looked out toward the sea. But how to tread soundlessly upon these grating pebbles? Luckily, though, the waves growled and moaned like the beasts denned beneath the streets of Rome, the ones being starved to eat criminals . . .

You are not a criminal, he told himself firmly. You're at the edge of the world. There must be laws for one to be a criminal, and this place—it's well beyond laws.

He placed each step just when a wave crashed, and so was muffled by water. He crept behind the house, clinging to its moon-chalked shadow, and so was camouflaged by light as well. Cloaked by water and light: the laws of nature embraced him, if the laws of men did not. Perspiring, he pushed on, moving carefully around the house. When he reached the stone table, something nudged at his head, and he ducked, clutching himself in mortal fear. Above him swung the old weathered basket.

He wrapped one hand around a rung of the ladder, and with this familiar act his stomach lurched. One hand, two, now a long foot, and he pulled himself up to the door.

The moon at that moment obligingly illuminated the bronze door handle, the two-tailed mermaid herself, with her tiny, perfect breasts and her slim arms curved around the tails drawn up at either side. He ran a thumb along a fish tail, along the minute scales and the tender plume at the end, along the lovely miniature belly and the supple swelling of her hips . . . He felt a ludicrous stirring.

Then at last: with his left hand clutching the ladder, he reached to the right and gripped the sill; wedging his toes between two planks, he peered in.

And what did he see but a white-skinned girl with long webby hair, twined, facedown, in crumpled linen, one dirty foot poking from the sheets. He perched there, gazing at her bare ivory calf, and suddenly wanted to touch her. She scratched her arm just then and flung herself over; Ovid held his breath, fingers gripping the sill—and then he saw that her mouth was bound.

A piece of green, gold-spotted silk had been tied tightly around her mouth—he could see how it pinched at her cheeks. Yet her hands were free: she scratched with one finger upon the sheet. She had tied the cloth herself. He felt himself thrilling. To keep herself quiet? But there was a forest between her and the next living soul. To keep something in, then? Or to keep something *out*?

Her brow, as she slept, became deeply furrowed. As he let his eyes rest upon her, he saw her hands slowly tense and fist. They moved over her chest, her nails digging into her palms. So was that how she bled? He strained to see closer. As he watched, transfixed, her hands fumbled at the cloth around her mouth; then abruptly they wrenched it away. Freed, her lips opened. He watched, his own lips pressed tight to keep in the sound of his hammering heart. But not a sound came from her. Instead she exhaled deeply, more than a sigh, as though ridding herself of all her breath, her being. She lay motionless, emptied, her lips parched.

Was she alive? He nearly jogged her by the shoulder, but pulled his hand back to the sill. A breeze gusted in then behind him, raising the hairs on his neck. A strange breeze, with a whiff of cold rot, as if it had drifted up from deep in the ground. He shivered, and as it passed through the window he heard a papery rustle and felt the touch of a silk cord on his hand. Goose bumps rose on his arm and hers, too, as the breeze reached her, lifting a strand of her hair; she opened her lips and breathed deeply in. And in that moment she seemed to alter: her face darkened with rage.

Yet that had been all, that night. She hadn't stirred further; she hadn't risen. He'd crept home at last, unsatisfied.

———

Ovid gazed at the silent flutter of insects dancing around the flame; idly he passed his hand through it, parting the insects in a swath. He smelled his hand and studied the oily black streak left on the side of his palm. It took a moment for the tiny creatures to recover, regroup, resume their private reeling.

"You'll burn," he informed one wisp fluttering too near the flame. He blew gently, sending it staggering toward the window. But after a moment it returned, determined. He watched it flare and then float to the table. Dabbing it up with a fingertip, he flicked it out the window. He wondered whether the creature's tiny spirit had burned along with its transparent wings and curling abdomen, whether its spirit was gaseous and might burn blue, and then simply disappear.

Breath, spirit: Ovid latched his long hands together. The breath the girl had taken, the cold, rotten breeze that had seemed suddenly to swirl in the room: he could see it now, animate. For *anima* meant breeze, breath, spirit, all together. And that was all words were, all a self was made of. Squinting to see beyond the wavering flame and through the rings into the darkness, he imagined what had entered her room as no simple breath but *figurative*. Perhaps it was something subtle that flew in out of this wild, vegetative landscape, some grim spirit of this place, which perched on her sleeping chest, breathed itself into her mouth, and thereby effected a change: an infusion of different character.

Are there such things in the air, which can breathe into you at night? He'd imagined it himself, in his story of Erysichthon and Hunger. His Hunger had been monstrous, all bone and running sore and want—she had flown in greedy Erysichthon's window, squatted on his chest, waited until his mouth opened wide in a snore, and then hideously breathed herself into him. Ovid realized now, with a thrilled shudder, that his Hunger had dwelled here, in the Caucasus. Again, *again* this girl embodied his characters—as if he'd conjured her himself.

Absurdus.

He rubbed his bare arms rapidly to smooth the roused fine hairs. Yet still he felt a chill, felt that old, old knot of guilt, as he neatly stacked his blank wax tablets, as he bound his sandals about his feet, as he blew out his lamp, and as he stepped from the ladder into the sinking grass.

He did not reach her house, that night. He was beyond the grasses and the cucumber field and at her edge of the dark bristling pines, leaning a moment against a trunk to shake some needles from his sandal, when he saw what he had sought.

The moon was waning, uneven, but still its light fell through the thin boughs, silvering the bark of the trees and pooling upon the sandy floor. As he paused, the woods seemed to grow live all around him; no longer hearing his own thrashing and gasps, he heard the trees, the breeze, the faint waves far away, tiny animal motions. Then he made out a low voice.

A pale figure crouched in a clearing, just before him. He flattened himself against the trunk and listened. A singsong, he thought, a low lullaby, with only the faintest rustling. Her furl of webby hair, her form bent and cradling in the moonlight. A child, she almost seemed, with a doll.

Then, to his shock, came a shrill animal scream. He saw just a flash—a whiteness, a raw redness—and a branch cracked beneath his foot and she was gone, streaking away ghostly in the woods.

Behind her he stood stunned, fixed to the tree, eyes round in the darkness, the scream and the image still flaring. He trembled. To picture her: crouched over the little furred creature, or feathered creature, or whatever it was, lullabying, cooing, and then—nails and teeth. Yet she didn't even know? Then how she ran. She'd stagger back to the stretch of pebbles, climb up her ladder, drop into bed. Tomorrow she'd wake up with the dreadful evidence. And run to wash it away.

He leaned against the tree, one hand clutching behind him. Breaking away a chip of bark, he rubbed it between his finger and thumb—it was like flayed, petrified flesh. *Daphne, Marsyas.* He let it drop to the ground. A girl who becomes something else, he thought, who has in her something *other*. Such a capacity for violence, and for violation . . .

As he stood there, his back against the rough mast of pine, moonlight at his feet, he could not help it: the idea began to take form. The idea of what he might do with this girl. From somewhere near the base of his spine the vision crept, slowly, chilling his blood, raising the hairs on his neck.

No. Quickly he pushed away from the tree and walked out of the woods, into the open air, to the reassuring sound of the waves. He made himself look at her little house, made himself free her from the net of his mind and place her back in the world. Chewing the inside of his mouth, he dropped onto the sand, behind the beach rose.

Then he noticed something in the sand by the shrub: a finger-size roll of half-burned papyrus, bound by a lock of singed glassy hair. Curious, he drew it out.

Some time later, as he reached his house and placed a hand upon his ladder, he saw a single gray feather floating, poised vertically, up into the sky.

How could he possibly resist this?

6

Every evening Xenia took out her knife, cut loose a poem and a lock of hair, pricked her finger, tilted her lamp, and, as the magical packet burned, whispered the *carmina* that floated up the beach, over the silvery tips of the trees, beyond the rivulet, to that stilted dark house. The spells would slip in the window, hover around his head, dart invisible into his sleeping mouth: they would make her be loved by the love-artist himself.

She knew she drew him. She knew he was watching her from behind the trees as she worked one day—and, what luck, an exorcism! Those admiring eyes upon her as she performed, leaving warmth like sun on her skin: it was absolutely new to her. She felt that hypnotizing gaze as she tied the boy to her ladder, as she brought out the smoking mastigia and lotus pith mixed with marjoram, as she wrote the stern command on the tin tablet and hung it around the boy's neck. Then the recitation, forward and backward, and the crucial blowing, all the way up his body twice without stopping for breath. At last the sulfur and bitumen explosion, to burn the monstrous thing out. Success!

All the while, upon her shoulders and arms, upon the backs of her calves as she knelt, upon her lips as she blew, roving through her floating hair, those eyes traveled like warm, knowing fingers. Her cheeks burned, her eyes glowed: she was lit to life.

He watched her not just that day but again, as if he could not help himself. She saw him there, the top of his sculptural head, and pretended not to see. When the bushes rustled and he was gone, she glided up her ladder, sat before the mirror, and studied herself, trembling. Yes, she drew him. But it was not just the spells, she suddenly thought: not just the hair, the burnt poems, the words. A tremulous pride began to glimmer inside her, and she gazed at her eyes, at the shadows of her throat, at her knowledgeable hands, and thought, It is *me* that he sees: what I am, what I do. There is something in me that he needs.

Then footsteps traveled back and forth between the two stilted houses, the one on pebbles and the one on the hillock, in the blowing grass. Her smaller footsteps hurried along the beach, sinking in the sucking sand as she urged on her whispered words, intent; his larger ones crept through the pine trees, upon the fallen needles. He looked in her window, he studied her chart and alembic, he read the charred words of his own smoldering poems, touched the sooty papyrus to his tongue, and imagined her flesh likewise melting. He gazed at her furtively from behind the trees and marveled at what he saw, and how effortless it was.

Until finally the day came when footsteps would have met plotting footsteps but for the narrow band of water that flowed between them, where the rivulet met the sea. It broke from the edge of the pine woods, and here, where it cut a path through the sand toward the surf, it had loosened the earth; several pines had fallen and lay like bridges, their roots now shaggy caves on either bank, their branches long arms endlessly wetted by the running waters.

Xenia was stooping at the rivulet's edge, heels on the crisp sandy bank, waiting for the delicious moment when it would give and she'd go sliding in. Behind her lay a long line of her footprints, the near ones filling with shining water in the afternoon sun. Crouching, she forgot, for the moment, her mission. The weak waves were collapsing to her left, the rising swells holding light. Boats of water hyacinth and clods of tangled grass whirled before her, swerving toward the surf.

At last the sandbank broke and she slid into the stream. Lurching to her feet, knee-deep, she shook out her wet dress and looked up. And that was when she saw him, on the other bank. He stood with his narrow head cocked, lit in the late-afternoon sky, his long monkey arms at his sides, the fingers of one hand playing upon an invisible instrument, footsteps winding away behind him. His long shadow lay on the flowing water's surface, streaming and streaming toward her.

He was smiling, Roman-gray eyes regarding her, his fingers still playing their private music. Then he threw back his head and laughed once, like crowing, his voice flying above the waves. He tossed away his instrument and splashed toward her through the stream.

7

Later, still tasting, still burning, Ovid ruminated. He lay on his bed, one long arm flung behind his head, the sky through the window glowing violet, a tangerine cloud drifting north. An early evening breeze blew from the sea, over the whistling grasses. Raising his hand, he let the air run through his fingers. He was pleasantly naked, his skin still heated and abraded, his clothes hanging dripping out the window, drenched and sandy. He would shake them like sails when they'd dried, see the salt and sand shower sparkling through the air.

Sails. With his eyes shut, and the breeze upon his hand, and the steady rhythmic breaking of the waves, he could be on the sea. Where he should be soon, he supposed . . .

His fingers played at the stinging little line of frayed skin on his shoulder. He wasn't sure when she'd done it, or with what: her nails, her teeth, a serrated shell? But he found it appealing; he'd give up a few drops of blood to catch hold of this mythical creature. It piqued.

The feel of her body, that flesh he'd studied so often through water and windows and moonlight: the memory of it swept through him like a wave as he lay there, and he caught his breath. He'd felt her body finally through streaming water, through sheer, clinging linen. Her childish belly, her hips—the thumbs of his two long hands gripping her there had met, and the feel of such slender plumpness and containment—it was like teeth sinking into sweet, salty fruit. His mouth had filled at once with water. He'd pulled her down at the dissolving edge of the rivulet and done it all right there, half in and half out of the rushing river, while the sand kept sliding away beneath them, dissolving into water itself.

He laid the back of his hand upon his sticky forehead and breathed in time with the waves until the beating in his throat died down. He had kept to himself a long time, he realized. The taste of her skin, of her curious, persimmon tongue! And such shocking natural skill—it was manifestly her first time, but what she seemed to *know*! God—again—that sense of being plumbed, nothing at all to be done . . . The way his hands, his tongue, had seemed to melt her. Again a finger strayed over the line of dried blood on his shoulder, and excitement, tenderness, and discomfort twitched inside him.

Afterward, he'd lounged like a river god in the flowing water, hyacinths tangling around his legs, and watched her tug her feet from the sand and pull her sopping clothing over her chafed white back. He looked up at her, warm sun on his jaw, smiling sleepily, squinting. "A witch," he said, "I think, aren't you?" She'd merely glanced at him with a curious smile and walked haughtily down the beach.

Haughty, *she*! She with her hands bloodied in the morning, her eyes completely bewildered. But she too was the creature who had crashed confidently from that pool; who apparently had one eye in the future; who, all this time, had been winding silky strands around his body; who had seemed there, in the water, to be inside his very skin, she'd known so precisely what to do, and when. Ovid examined the finger that had brushed his scratch, half expecting it to smoke.

And he still could scarcely believe it. For when he looked at her, it was so easy: words whispered themselves in his ear, scenes floated before his eyes. So much easier than with Corinna, from whom he'd had to rip what he saw flickering in her eyes and mouth, dancing in the shadows on her body; from whom he'd had to steal what he needed for his *Loves*. But this fabulous girl . . .

Afterward, after Xenia tugged her feet from the sucking sand and pulled her wet dress over her body, she walked down the beach, the low sun lighting her right arm, her right leg. Her head was burning with excitement. As she dumped her clothes on the stone table and went and stood in the sea, it kept coming back to her in explosions.

She saw again his eyes upon her as he came lunging through the water. Laughing eyes, laughing as he fell splashing to his knees, laughing as he kept coming. Laughing eyes and laughing hands, laughing clever fingers. They'd wrapped right around her—and the thought of those long, intelligent, *famous* hands on her untouched young hips stunned her even now. The hands that had written those poems—the poems that all the world knew, the poems that had tied knots in her heart—the same hands had held her through her billowing wet dress. And with those hands at her hips, the paired thumbs nudging, it was as if something unwound inside her, a gold snake slinking free. The water rushed and swirled all around; the sand beneath her slid away; her hair flowed in the silty water; his skin and mouth were delicious to her ravenous tongue; and with his fingers dabbling and tickling and teasing, it was like honey slowly melting, like wax turned clear and liquid, sweet.

Xenia closed her eyes, breathed three times, and opened them again. She placed her hands upon the water that slowly rose and lowered. A cow stood nearby, its tail floating on the surface, and gazed at her with its soft brown eyes. Xenia drew a circle on the water and said to the cow, "Ovid." A gull skimmed by. "Publius Ovidius Naso," she said. Just saying the name made her feel she possessed the man, the very world he figured.

She shook her head. Gathering up an armful of seaweed, she carried it over the beach, laid it upon her drying-rack, and, as it dripped upon the pebbles, popped a few pods, smelling its saltiness. *Phycos thalassion* . . . Once it was crisp, she would grind it with her egg-shaped stone, feel the pleasing crunch and crackle, until it was finer than sand, bloodred. A marvelous powder, a durable pigment, brushed on wounds and Roman walls and papyri, creating purity and art.

Ovid. She shut her eyes. Although she had touched his damp chest and felt the solidity of his hip bones, although she'd tasted the olive flavor of his tongue and the salty sweat of his wrists, she'd seen that he was spectacular—a dragonfly, a god. She had *seen* it: how he would be borne up over the crowds, how gold would fall upon him in showers. He would return triumphant to Rome, more triumphant than he had ever been. A shiver ran from her throat to her knees. For if she were there, beside him? To be *loved* by the love-artist . . .

To be his subject, his muse.

The thought had no sooner materialized than it seized her. Yes: he and she were perfectly paired—magical, transformative. The poet and the heroine. Her *carmina*, all her brilliance, should be made famous by his.

8

After that, Xenia streamed into the whorls of Ovid's elegant ears. Beneath his tracing fingertips and eyes she lay as if filled by a god, her tongue suddenly alive. She told the secrets of planetary metals, the best techniques for sending dreams, what she'd seen shimmering around whom, how she never drowned cats, as was usual for enacting wishes, but had developed subtler means; she hinted about color, and light, and the quintessence. Once or twice she looked up, surprised, when he seemed hardly to believe her.

"Of course that's true," she said. "I saw it." He only blinked with those Roman-gray eyes before resuming his invisible writing upon her skin.

She told of how the male fern fingers might make you invisible, of how she'd blown that boy clean of a demon and burned it safely up. She revealed secrets of breath and how one must be careful; she even disclosed her pink fish-skin bag, but this he seemed to understand. "So no one will make use of what's in it," he said, and she nodded.

On and on she went. Her singsong curled in his ears, many

of her secret spells, the alchemical rule itself—to control every subtle thing and penetrate each solid . . . All the while his fingers traced over her skin, pausing sometimes as he gazed into her yellow-and-gray eyes, wandering through her hair.

"Our work is similar," he said once.

"*Carmina*," she whispered. He breathed the word in like smoke.

Carmina, love poems, magic. She pondered him, and had him tell of Rome and Augustus, and how he had stood on the banks of the Tiber, burning his poems one by one.

"He thought I mocked his laws," said Ovid.

She thought of laws—the laws of nature, the laws of men, the laws of grim Augustus—and wondered whether fear would keep Ovid from taking her with him.

"Little laws," she murmured after a moment, and now he pondered her.

His words wound into her ears as well, as he recited to her from his *Metamorphoses*, his eyes half shut, voice low. *I'll write about bodies transfigured* . . . She entered a world of stones that became as tender as skin, feathers that sprouted from fingertips, hair coarsening to brambles and twigs, flesh hardening again to lifeless stone, girls flung into the sky as stars. Girls ran, frantic, letting their legs melt to water, rather than be seized; a boy was left hanging in sheer air, his feathers fallen away, his thin arms clutching at nothing; a boy dissolved with love for his own untouchable beauty.

It was all just as she'd seen it, when she watched Ovid from behind the rock: all those tiny images hovering about him. She looked up as his voice spun on, while outside the evening clouds towered with burning gold edges. Xenia held up a hand and turned it around, expecting it to sprout brilliant blue feathers, to break into pink bud, into leaf.

"You like it," he said after a time. "You like my promiscuous darling." She smiled in the dimming light, and he turned to her, his eyes as gray as the sky behind him.

"But the next one," he whispered, "will be . . . singular." She felt her heart grow still.

Twice she woke to find him sitting in the moonlight with his eyes fixed upon her. He stared a moment before becoming himself, and ran a finger from her neck to her hip.

After two weeks she realized that she'd forgotten the piece of green silk she tied around her mouth, but now it seemed unnecessary.

One evening, as they lay upon the bed and a cool sea breeze blew in, Ovid opened his eyes and sniffed; near the window something rustled. He got up, abstracted, looked out at the darkening sea, and sat down at his table. His shoulders settled at an angle, his dark head intent between them.

From the bed, Xenia let her eyes move slowly around him. Over the comings and goings of the waves and the wind through the grasses, she listened to him write. His stylus whispered; it rasped; it grew quicker, more measured. A cloak fell about him when he worked, opaque, smelling something of incense. She concentrated on his bent back, his head, that long hand rapidly writing, the muscles taut at his knuckles. He would not say what he wrote, and she would never ask: sacred. But as he worked she listened, to see if she could *hear* the words as they passed from mind to wax. The waves rolled on; his hand kept moving over the black tablet. And as she gazed and listened she suddenly saw that what he wrote now would be his most powerful work, better even than his *Metamorphoses*.

At once there was a silence, as if her epiphany had made his concentration waver, a breeze bending a flame. Then he turned and looked at her. She looked at him, but at that moment she knew he didn't see her—or that he saw her not as one sees a person but as an artist dissects a subject. He did not speak, and neither did she, not that whole long moment. She held herself still and imagined herself as a magical lantern, her secrets coming to life by his hand.

Outside, the breeze picked up, an autumn breeze, blowing west.

That night she sat at her table, staring into the flame and at the shapes of the shadows it cast, and thought, He must say that he is going and that he wants me to come.

After she had gone home Ovid sat on, peering out into the dark. This icy, melting, blood-extracting creature, this girl with marvelous eyes . . . Yes, he thought. The way she turns herself to me . . . She wants herself plundered, transcribed.

The grasses outside were whistling, blowing, streaming toward the sea. A gust of wind made him suddenly alert. He must go, he realized, before the weather changed. Over all those seas: he must get back to Rome. To his house, his life, his future—to see how that brilliant book had been received. He looked up, impatient, his body suddenly itching to be where his mind had flown. So tedious, this baggage, arms and legs and bellies and so on.

He rubbed his hands together, cracked his knuckles over

the flame. The thing to do would be to ride to Dioscurias, find out when there would be a boat, and arrive at last in Rome, triumphant.

Closing his eyes, Ovid let himself fall back upon the clouds of his envisioned success. There he was, striding through a triumphal arch into Rome, all the women in murex and saffron and lilac dresses crying out, waving, laughing, throwing flowers into the air. He could see the little blossoms tumbling slowly in the brilliant sun, the long bare arms of the women, their dark-lined eyes, their laughing, reddened mouths. He could see his friends, tearful with the plangency of his words! He could see his rivals, with cool, twisted smiles.

But not just *them*, he corrected himself, focusing anew: much more important, a *patron*. A wonderful new patron! A whole phalanx of patrons, vying to win him! Coins flying! Not just blossoms in the air but showers of gold! And above it all: Augustus, pleased at last.

After a moment Ovid opened his eyes and compelled himself to see the real surfaces, the writing table, his bag, his stylus. He compelled himself to hear the steady, sobering rhythm of the sea, to recollect its weight and the volumes of its waters.

And this icy, melting, blood-extracting creature?

Of course he was taking her with him. She was crucial to him now.

Again Corinna appeared, her lovely face before his eyes, her nude body as she'd risen angrily from bed. *You are a crow! You watch, and wait, and then fly at me to snatch what you want to use.* He had pondered her words as he lay gazing at her, and had for a moment felt his nose becoming a hard beak, his skin turning to glossy black feathers. But she was still looking at him, standing there, weight on one hip, her body barred with shuttered light. *Do you actually like that?* she asked. He smiled, and she stared, laughed a laugh as brittle as gold foil, and turned away.

But you know I love you, he said then, his voice in his own ears pleading, so that—what else could he do?—he laughed, loud and barking.

She fixed him with those eyes flecked like travertine. *You don't know the difference between love and art. Between loving and stealing.*

He stared at her adored face. And again—what else could he do?—he laughed. He left. Later he floated in the warm baths, and he knew that he did know the difference, but it kept drifting from view.

That was the beginning of the end. He could no longer help himself; even that day he stole for his *Loves,* turning it into the famous scene in the bedroom with shuttered light.

I don't know, she screamed near the end, *whether you're creating me or raping me! Stop! Stop watching!*

And then: *You are Pygmalion's opposite. You've polished me dead.*

Oh, but even that: even after she'd finally left him, after he'd heard his own hoarse voice that night on the street, after he'd gone out savaging and written his *Art of Love*—even after those dark years, the vicious book, and all the women, he'd stolen again from Corinna. *Pygmalion's opposite.* From her words had sprung his *Metamorphoses.*

Yet, he thought now, resting his chin on his latched fingers as he listened to the whistling wind, Yet you will do it again.

It angered him, the knot he felt, and he flung his hands apart and stood up. Yes, he thought as he paced: I will. I *want* this Xenia. And it's different, because she agrees. You can see it in every motion, in those inflamed eyes! She absolutely gives herself.

But did she know to what?

He opened the door, his nose to the keen wind blowing toward Rome, and suddenly thought of his earliest days there, when, as a boy, he'd come from the countryside to study law, determined to please his father and follow the honorable Roman path.

Which he could have done. He had set himself to it with burning eagerness, hungry to learn and see everything. But after only a year he'd made a discovery. He'd been pacing somberly before his masters, piecing together his argument, when something lit inside him. It was like that, a flash, a sudden fire, and all at once it seemed his tongue could do anything: spin arguments around like a top, convict a man and then acquit him, topple his own logic. He could build up his case, weave a tight net of reason, and then laughingly shake it out empty. His tongue had a life of its own. A green tongue, a devil's tongue; his eyes burned above it, enthralled. And though he felt the horror in the eyes of his masters, he'd been unable to stop.

He'd abandoned the law, but not this terrible skill. It had run like a silver thread through all he'd done since—through his wicked *Art of Love*, showing how to woo and then to abandon; through his clever defense of the poem as well; and brightly, darkly, through the *Metamorphoses*: when Myrrha argued that it was no more a crime for her to sleep with her father than it was for a filly to mate with its sire—*Human nature has made malignant laws, laws that go against nature!*— or when Byblis justified her lust for her brother by citing incestuous precedents among the gods . . . Passionate figures, their logic flawless: Ovid's words in their mouths turned the world inside out.

So was he using this skill even now?

He shut his eyes and flew in his mind over the seas, Xenia's hand clasped in his, and placed her in his house at the foot of the Palatine, in the rooms just across the garden. He could see how the sunlight would slant through the windows; he could see her moving about, concocting. He flew with her then into the streets of Rome. And the things she needed, and the subjects? He shifted his weight, uncomfortable. Pharmakal, magical, alchemical . . . He wondered what *sorcery*, technically, was. But it was like adultery, abortion—who would ever know. Or care. Preposterous! He flung out his arm, into the blowing dark night. *Little laws.*

Ovid shut the door and looked at his small room, suddenly so foreign. He pulled on a mantle and began to pack.

Corinna had wanted only to live. But this Xenia, he thought: she wants to live *on.*

9

The next day he came and stood before her, conscious of his height and the shadow he cast, and said, "I want you to come with me." He breathed it into her hair and watched as it rose, electric, all around her. He leaned so close that he felt he was breathing her in with his sensitive, avaricious nostrils. "You're coming with me," he whispered. His satchel hung from his shoulder, packed with all his tablets; he was riding to find a freighter.

"To Rome," she said, on the blowing sand. She watched as he swung a long leg over the back of the horse and righted himself aloft.

"Did you know I was equestrian rank? Augustus himself gave me a horse." He laughed. "Yes, of course, to Rome."

"Where I will do my work," she said.

"Of course," he replied, too jolly.

"And the law?"

He smiled, feeling his teeth very white. "It hardly stops adulterers. One just doesn't do it in the street. Makes the demand all the greater."

She regarded him then, a long moment.

"I need you," he said suddenly. Her head was aslant, hair blowing in the breeze, those strange eyes showing how she burned to be known. He added, more softly, "I think you need me, too."

She smiled then, her curious smile. And there passed between them a silent look, an unspoken exchange, ungraspable as mercury, welding.

Then he was off, satchel thumping at his side, horse's hooves kicking up sand, sky-blue cloak billowing. He would be back within a few days, he had told her, and she must be ready to go. For you never knew when a ship would be heading against the Black Sea currents to slip, laden with sturgeon, caviar, linen, and timber, back out into the world.

After he was gone, after she watched that fabulous figure gallop away, Xenia stood there, floating.

She ran home, ran in and out of her house, shaking linen, wrapping up little alabaster boxes, tucking cloths and dried leaves around her athanor and alembic, gathering knives and packets of powders, laying them in her painted wooden chest, carefully rolling her chart. Her house of black pine: it seemed so small, already forgotten beneath her air-swimming feet. For she was being carried aloft—amid showering gold and purple silks and raised hands and shouting—floating bedecked above a mob, like Cleopatra in triumph with Antony.

To Rome, to the world, to life. With him.

That afternoon she slept—sunken, hot-afternoon sleeping—her packing done, her little house dismembered and hollow, even her bronze mermaid carefully prized from the door.

In her sleep, Xenia seemed to drift on the waves that rose and broke outside her window. Her skin was damp, moisture gathering at the roots of her hair, and again she fell into her dream. The sky was dark, swirling; cold water rose beneath her, pooling around her small limbs in the basket. Before her in the darkness hovered that face, the face she saw only in this dream. White, ghostly, with eyes so tortured, with the bloody mouth that almost smiled, the trembling pale hand near her cheek. The water rose, and Xenia rose with it; she felt the wet weave of the basket's edge in her clinging fingers and that gentle touch on her face. But then—the shocking shove, the violent surge, and she was pushed, screaming and begging and alone, out onto the dark sea.

Ovid returned a few days later, breakneck, eyes as wild as the frothing horse's. He'd had extraordinary luck: a merchant ship was bound for Rome; they must depart the next morning.

It was drizzly that dawn, full of autumn and seeping cool mist. Ovid's hand was damp around Xenia's as they stepped into the boat that would row them and their baggage beyond the pebbles. The sea was opaque, dead gray; the sky, too, was lightless, giving nothing.

Xenia looked back over the iron waves to the stretch of pebbles, her little house, the misty layers of wet green hills. Two girls stood on the shore, staring. Xenia lifted a hand, but they did not move, so she let it fall again. She touched the basket on her lap and looked at him. He caught her glance and lightly laughed, a thin sound in the wind, his face greenish with the boat's rough rocking.

PART TWO

1

At the prow of the ship rose the head of a swan, with a black-lined, devious eye; a crisscross rail ran around the deck; and at the stern was the carved head of a woman with flowing blue-black hair. The one who'd fallen in love with the god disguised as a swan, Xenia thought, the one whose body had been enveloped by his white wings, her bare legs tickled by his black webbed feet.

Passengers slept in small linen tents, the few women in one zone of the deck, the men in another, with a length of old sail stretched between them. People came and went at the various ports as the ship bore around the southern edge of the Black Sea, barrels of goods loaded or unloaded at each stop. The women spent the days on little stools, staring out at the rolling sea, chatting, narrating the sights that went by. Over there you might see where Marsyas's skin had been hung once Apollo had pulled it from his quivering red muscles; there you'd find Helen's bracelet; here you could view the bones of a giant; there the jaw of a whale. From the other end of the deck came the sounds of men as they played dice, their shouts of *Venus!* or

Dogs! for high or low throws blowing back to the women. Xenia saw Ovid among the men, tall, his head tanned and tossed back just then, laughing.

Night on the Black Sea. Rope and sail snapped, wood creaked, water heaved. Leaning over the railing, she saw once, as she saw these things, a young boy sinking. His long greenish leg stabbed at the water, his tunic ballooning slowly around him, one arm stretched above. His hair flowed and swayed like seaweed, and from the purse tied about his waist fell coins, turning and glinting as they sank. They would be eaten by the deeper waters, where there was no oxygen and where metals and cloths were dissolved, yet flesh was left whole. Far above him the waves receded, and finally, in the darkness, his body bumped upon the seabed. It would never be consumed. Instead, it would gently roll, pale and naked, forever alone upon the lifeless seafloor. An arm dangling, colorless hair swaying, cold fingernails leaving wavering trails in the sand.

Night on the sea, night after night. The stars glittered, silent and cold, blacked out now and then by invisible sails. Upon the stretch of cloth between men and women moved shadows, lengthening and fading, sliding over each other, being drawn sharp and close until the screen bulged with the dark touch of a hand.

Before dawn many mornings, Xenia crawled out and gripped the railing, leaned over, and retched. She let her head hang, her hair whipping about her unclean mouth, until the traces were lost in the waves. All around was an oily gray light, a smell of salt and iron. She poured a little water from the jar, splashed her face, and noticed again that there was never any blood on her hands.

There had been no blood at all. In the weeks they'd been

sailing, and for several weeks before, there'd been no blood on her hands, none sticky between her legs. She gazed up at the carved swan. Ovid slept somewhere beyond the screen, where even the married men slept. *Married*: a word that meant nothing to her, a word as lifeless as *law*. When that blue-haired woman had let the swan's huge wings enfold her, when she'd felt his downy white neck slide softly between her breasts and over her excitable stomach, she'd never thought of marriage. Children born of golden eggs: what had they to do with ordinary, sublunary marriage?

It came to earth so very rarely, this divinity. Gold showered through the window of a high bedroom, startling a girl with plump thighs; the moon chanced upon a boy asleep in the woods and gathered him up in her shining arms; a dove flew through a window in a ray of light, plunging toward a girl's breast; and there was the swan, and the white bull, and the breeze sent by Amor . . . She could feel it now, that breeze, tickling her ankles, flitting at her calves and the fine down on her thighs, lightly lifting her dress, billowing around her, carrying her aloft. To Rome, to the world, to life. With him.

Ovid gazed out at the soft blue night, smelling the sea, hearing the ropes groan and the wood creak. He thought of the hold, full of fish eggs tightly packed in salt and buried in the cold, wet sand that was the boat's ballast. Strange to think of the hull, so deep in the inhospitable sea but laden with the sea's own sand, as this ship carried him, all those billions of tiny eggs, and this marvelous girl from her imaginary land to real Rome. Through the torn sail, Ovid watched her tent. Would her hands part the linen and precede her, trancelike, out upon deck? The tent was like a chrysalis, he thought, with something wrapped in silk and leaves inside, sleeping, just beginning to transform into what had been hidden within it all along.

Xenia's tent shifted, and he leaned forward. He had seen her stagger to her feet at dawn and lurch toward the railing, lean over, try to stifle her sickened sounds, wipe her mouth with the back of her hand. Seeing it twice was enough; this was no ordinary seasickness. A crucial transformation.

For a moment he let rise before him the thought of what he planned to do with this extraordinary girl.

Tragedy was a higher form. It had called him and called him, but he had never yet dared it.

He had not planned to find her, with her arts, in that place of all places; he had not planned to find her, or have her, or bring her back, like this.

But how could he possibly resist such a gift?

At dawn he looked through the torn sail again, holding it parted with his fingers. There she was, leaning against the balustrade. Her head hung, her hair flicked at her face, her hands lay on the railing. Then she lifted her head and cocked it, and he knew that she was seeing something no one else could see.

Last week, as they passed through the Bosporus, Xenia had smiled and said, very quietly, something that had stunned him: that his next work would be his most powerful, better even than the *Metamorphoses*, which itself would be considered . . . But she had not gone on, only smiled. Though he'd stared at her, he hadn't dared ask more. Having tossed her gifts, she'd turned, eyes glowing with pride.

Imagine if she could really see such a thing!

He could not believe it. Absurd.

He peered at her now, fingering the frayed edges of the linen as if it were her skin and, by peeling it back, he might see inside her, see if what she'd said was true—and more: see what would become of him. Not *himself*: he didn't care about that. How he would die, and when: no matter. No, it was *after* he cared about. After all those years—the thousands of years and millions of people still to come, who would tread unthinking upon the dense earth that would settle over his bones. The thought that he might simply be lost beneath it all, forgotten— this he could not bear.

At that moment, up on the Palatine, Julia was crouching on the floor of a chamber lit by just one small lamp. The floors of her rooms were always intricate, and this one was mosaicked as a seabed, with pink corals, water grasses that almost waved, and darting yellow fish.

Julia was crouching, a sheen of moisture on her tense, drawn face, her dark hair having fallen somewhat from its coiffure; a long golden needle had been removed from the coils and braids. She was holding it in her hand and passing it slowly, almost lovingly, through the flame of the lamp. Abruptly, she blew the flame out.

Eyes shut in the dark, her thoughts twisted together, pulsing and reddening with the sudden sharp stab. Her mother: she thought hard of her mother, pacing a room on an island off Neapolis. Suddenly Julia could smell them, her mother's famous adulteries, sex mixed with blood and her own pain-sharp perspiration. The smell of sex: it sickened her. Her body jerked with a fresh stab, but she continued, tightening her fingers around the needle. She must hold it firmly, slide it with

precision, up and deeply in. Drops of red blood traveled down
the gold needle and fell upon the tiny mosaic squares beneath
her sweating thighs, upon the lovely swishing sea with its
anemones and urchins.

Continue. With one hand she held herself open, fingers
pressing the little jungle of sweat-soaked hair; with the other
she forced in the needle. *Oh, god, Mother! Look what I have to
do, look what you've left me to do.*

But she knew that wasn't fair. Her mother had done her best.
She would not.

Oh, she thought, the gods did this sort of thing, too, didn't
they, the gods from whom her grandfather insisted his own
flesh had sprung. Uranus stuffed all his newborn children back
into their mother's aching womb like a game bird, stuffed them
there in greed and fright—for one was destined to outdo him.
And surely enough one did: crammed inside his mother's
womb, when his father next entered, he tore the monstrous
penis off. With their mother unstoppered, out the children
tumbled and swam, the castrator first among them. Out at last
in the bright world, he swung his father's severed organ around
and around his head, triumphant, the thing gray and shriveled
already, its loose, sticky skin still quivering from its shuddering
disappointment. He threw it out to sea. As it swung in the air,
drops of futile semen flew from one pulsing end, drops of hot
blood from the other. The semen fell into the water and was
born again as passion—but the blood fell upon the beach, and
there it seethed and rose up as Furies, the living rage between
parents and children who deny each other their lives.

After a time Julia became dizzy, weak; her cold bare foot
slipped on the bloody floor. But surely she must have done it;
she must have punctured the hated baby. She sat, dropping her

body onto the wet floor, heedless of her dress in the blood. Leaning to one side, she vomited, and then let her head hang, her hands wet and sticky, a stench all around her.

Now there was a tapping at the door of her chamber, and a bar of quavering light. A soft cry, a flurry of clean linen, and soothing hands were all upon her. Julia had excellent slaves. They'd mop everything up and burn her dress, as they'd done before. They'd smuggle in the well-paid physician. Her body would be healed, and all the evidence would be removed, that and the wretched little parasite itself, its gobbets of flesh thrown away. They knew never to tell, never a word to anyone, anywhere; Julia must seem ever compliant. But then she would do it again. The blood, the pain, the risk: it was nothing. She'd smile despite any pain, so long as she inflicted it upon Augustus as well—the more exquisitely so, as he had no idea how she hated him.

2

It was an autumn dawn when the ship finally glided toward Ostia, a smoky morning, the air hovering vaporous upon the dull water. Ovid, savage with stubble and long shell-like nails, stood against the rail in the breeze and looked toward the hazy land. They'd left the Black Sea more than a month before; they'd sailed easily over the Aegean (past islands of hovering Harpies), across the Ionian, through the Strait of Messina (Scylla's *dentata* lair), along the coast to Neapolis (where the Sirens gnawed upon men), and finally to where the water grew cloudier, where the Tiber and all the refuse of Rome poured out into the sea.

Ovid considered his dirty nails, quite foreign. To be in Rome, he thought; to be back in the polished world. To learn— at once he felt sick—how his *Metamorphoses* was being received. For it would be out now, unveiled just this week. Could he believe her tormenting hints? Yet how marvelous if she *knew* . . . At that thought the wind picked up, sails sucking and flapping, ropes groaning against timber, water sloshing at the boat's flanks. He pressed his lips together and forced away any thoughts that might wreck the ship, or wreck his bitterly strong hopes.

The land before them was now struck with light, blue broke out overhead, and sounds from the shore could just be caught on the breeze. All the passengers' eyes flew up to watch a gull as it coasted upon a stream of air. Squinting up, too, Ovid thought of his Daedalus and imagined those gray and yellow feathers falling from the small body, leaving it flailing and bare in the sky. Reckless thought! Anxiously, he looked to land and calculated the distance from ship to shore and the possibility of swimming. The bird at that moment dived to the right—splendid omen!—leaving only a ring of froth.

Smells came then, warm and fecund. A school of blood-eyed jellyfish floated by, tumbling beneath the prow or propelling themselves away with clear wings; gazing down at them, he saw again his Medusa. He saw his Glaucus in the swells, and his watery Arethusa, and his lovely Galatea—all his ambiguous creations, gliding and looking up at him with expectant, questioning eyes; he bit his teeth together and forced his ambition down. Now the port was drawing near, with the shapes of ships and buildings, and on the upper deck the last lamb cried out, having smelled earth and sweet air, only to have its throat swiftly slit, its blood caught up in a basin, in gratitude for the arrival.

Then the gangplank was swaying over the yellow water, there was the crush and the noise, the jammed breasts and bellies and satchels. Ovid pushed through, his head above all the other heads that were matted or curled, flaxen or black, braided or shaved to waxy skull. His nose felt sharp and he was excited nearly to sickness, one arm stretched out above him like a general, as he led the way to the boys struggling with chests and bags. He inhaled the smoky air, feeling himself borne above this sea of people. Fingers pointed, mouths whispered, eyes were fixed upon him—and all the crowd seemed suddenly an audience, witnessing his triumphant return. He could sense it; he could smell it: success!

He was sure of it! He gestured, one long hand flung into the air, as if it would fly away. And at that moment, his eyes stinging with tears, he could almost *see* it, as if he were Xenia and the world had pulled back its veils and given him a glimpse of the future—he could almost see this very place centuries later, nothing left but a dull blowing field: yet emerging from it as from underwater was he, Ovid, his head and his clever long hand, enduring.

"*Absurdus*," he whispered into the din. You are thinking of those buried statues around Athens; the world does not draw back its veils for *you*. You will be as deep underground as the rest of them.

All at once he was hollow. His hand fell back into the crowd; his head, too, seemed to go under, under all the coils and braids and mops of hair, all the sweat and reeking oil. He panicked and turned wildly, searching for Xenia—his charm, his secret, this girl who had the folds of his future tucked up like damp new wings inside her. He should have been holding her hand, he should have carried her over this rude mob! When he found her, floating slowly with the crowd, her eyes were fixed on his, her unsettling eyes, her lips parted in that quizzical smile, and he felt himself once more struck by that look with a jolt that ran from his throat to his knees.

Then they were rattling in a hired wagon up the long main street of Ostia, over the paving stones slick with blood, oil, fish guts, vegetable slime, through rows of hanging chickens and

heads of pigs and several watchful monkeys, mountains of cab-
bage, onions, garlic, bread; and all the shouting, toothless
faces—Ovid drank it in, this unruly life. He noticed how people stared at Xenia beside him, and he turned to her, squeezing
her hand or her leg; otherwise his long finger extended before
them, as if to point, or to pull them greedily along.

Soon they'd left Ostia and were traveling over the dry brown
fields with their cypresses and umbrella pines; at nightfall they
approached with a thundering thrill the famous hills, the magnificent city itself. And as they passed under the Ostian arch,
into the din of Rome's nighttime traffic, Ovid shut his eyes
until the tears nearly came, and he imagined again—willed
almost into being—that this was, finally, his triumph.

An hour later, Xenia was standing, enormously excited, in the
middle of her bedroom. After the endless glinting seas and
brown fields, suddenly she'd landed in this ornate house, in this
miraculous room; she felt her hands might pass through the
walls. Crouching, she ran her fingers down the curving slim
claw of a table leg; she studied the underwater scene on a wall
and the waving blue mosaic at her feet. *Rome!*

She went to a window. Her hand doming the oil flame, she
looked across the garden toward the dark other half of the
house, where Ovid's floating lamp had disappeared once he'd
left her in the hands of the old housekeeper, Persilla. His knee
had been jogging, his eyes bright, his hand clutching her leg as
they rode into the city, as they trotted along the river and finally
skirted the villa-crusted hills. He seemed even sleeker and taller
beside her, his eyes illuminated like the moon by the sun.

His house was between two hills, at the foot of the Palatine.

Persilla had greeted them, a mothlike old woman with milky eyes, who barely spoke but fluttered about her tasks, slight and ashen as the Sibyl shrinking in her jar. The atrium dripped as they passed through it; a little boy—the cook's—stood watching them from the edge of the impluvium, waving his arms slowly like a bird, his black hair shaved close to his square, bluish scalp. There was Lida, a plump girl with wild bear's eyes, and a thin, pocked boy, Lazar. Several rooms and halls branched off from the atrium, at the far end of which, behind a tall black screen, was Ovid's study; beyond that lay the garden, rimmed by a portico, with a new wing of private rooms to the right and one with the dining rooms to the left. Xenia was to live in the new quarters, Ovid himself in the older part of the house. The smells of the garden drifted in her window—its dark moisture, the bitterness of boxwood, faint lavender, lemon—and the fountain gently murmured; up on the hill the great temple glowed; through it all hung Rome's nighttime din.

She took off her dress and got into bed. The bedding was fresh and soft, and she drew her bare feet up into it, melting with pleasure. She blew out her lamp and lay there, rocking on the surface of Rome. How could she possibly sleep? When she shut her eyes, she still saw the glowing eyes of the street lamps, the luminous temple on the hill, Ovid's moonlit profile as he had turned to her, smiling, the passing city reflected in his eyes. Her last thought before drifting off was, What he makes of me must . . . be heroic.

3

The first days in Rome were all unpacking, settling, having haircuts and shaves, soothing disturbed, sea-tossed stomachs. Ovid's long manicured fingers trailed proprietarily along the frescoed walls—the black and gold architectural images painted in his bedroom, the grottoes along the hallway, the mythic scenes in red and moss green in the atrium and the dining room. Nymphs' peach thighs, blue-scaled fish, slavering hounds, satyrs: comforting creatures, beings of art, so like the figures in his marvelous book.

His book: he froze, remembering it, his fingers sticking to the wall, as salty waves of apprehension crashed through him. He ground his teeth to control them. Then, after a moment, his bare feet moved again with determined pleasure over the mosaicked floors, over scenes of sea monsters and abductions of girls by bull or cloud, *over* the dancing skeleton framed in the center of his black-and-white bedroom. He pondered the little skull and bones, sometimes, as his feet brushed over it; he noted Xenia noting that he did, as she lay nude and curious in his bed.

Many of the furnishings had been given, others he'd chosen,

but nothing was there by chance. His passion for artful things was terrible. As he gazed upon a painting or vase, he was utterly overtaken by that love of objects that only the mind or eye can devour, leaving the tongue loose and hankering. "It's really the only thing, isn't it?" he said to Xenia, and he felt his Daedalus eyes skimming high over the seas of the unhewn, the unwrought.

That marble could be carved and polished to take on the gleam and tenderness of flesh; that silks could be so tinted, crushed in his hand; that walls and table legs and even the smallest bronze weight could be wrought to serve both function and art; that food itself could be so sculpted: sometimes he could scarcely bear the splendor of it all, even thirty years since he'd first come to Rome, ruddy and rude from the country. He saw Xenia now as he had been then, running her finger with deep interest over a painted wisp of sheer apricot cloth, over the silver tendons of a tripod's lion leg.

He studied her, those first few days, as she moved about the house and stood in the garden, looking out toward the city with excitement tremulous in her limbs. He squinted sometimes, observing her, as she spoke her uneven Latin with Persilla and the others. They kept a distance instinctively, as if there were something about her, a screen. Yet they were fascinated: he'd seen Lida with her uncouth eyes ponder Xenia whole minutes, and Lazar flushed, his neck like chicken skin, if she merely turned his way. Her eyes, no doubt. Her coloring, her hair. Was she foreign everywhere? Persilla took Xenia in with one look, glanced at Ovid, and went back to her tasks.

He had not shown Xenia the city yet; he himself had not gone out, and she was still too unsettled, needing always to be near a bowl. Besides, he thought, she required presenting, whenever the two of them should appear . . . in triumph. He let himself think it, once again, shutting his eyes, floating above the heads of the crowd. Then, more calmly, he eyed her. She was in the garden, crouched over some rosemary, examining the soil, her dress hiked up to her thighs. For a moment he toyed with the familiar trope: the barbarian in the city. He considered the image from several angles and then crumpled it, tossed it away. No: she needed clothes, presentation.

A foreign look. Egyptian, or Syrian, or, at the very least, Greek? Something altogether Eastern? No: with her extreme fairness, none of those would do. Yet the sorts of things that might apply—northern cloaks, bearskins—seemed too barbaric for her complexity.

A puzzle. She stood up then, the sun flowing right through her dress, and he felt a sudden warmth, a weakening. Only veils, he decided, sheer like water itself, as he had first seen her, would do.

Four days after they'd arrived there was still no word, and he was in a paroxysm of anxiety, his body rigid, sheened in sweat. He lay in bed and with straining white eyes entreated any spirit that hovered nearby to please let him have what he wanted, to please let Xenia be right. He willed so hard that he almost felt his *genius*, his beating life itself, slip from his ears and go flying red and desperate up the Palatine to where that cold marble man sat.

On the fifth day, he could no longer bear it.

So, leaving Xenia muffled in silk and the women's anxious, pinning hands, Ovid, freshly clipped, shaved, oiled, and cloaked, finally went into town.

Marcus first! Publisher, gourmet, gourmand—the same greedy glow came to his eyes whether what lay before him was papyrus or feast, so long as it was *superb*. Ovid's heart beat violently, and he felt slippery slitherings in his knees; he cracked his knuckles loudly as he approached Marcus's house on the Esquiline and rapped on the door. Boisterous Marcus, his eyes damp with emotion, enfolded him in his butcher's arms. Then all the chatter—the journey, the dangers, what had gone on in Rome—until finally Ovid pushed it aside.

"My book." At which Marcus slipped away, so graceful for so round a man, somehow slipped from Ovid's vision, and began fussing somewhere about something.

"Ah yes," came his voice. It seemed, it did seem, that there had been some unusual interest. Not clear yet if the interest was positive . . .

"Who, Marcus?"

"Well, the Palatine. An early copy was sent up."

The Palatine! Which part of the Palatine? Ovid leapt to his feet, leapt from the house, went leaping up the Palatine. His knees felt like a camel's as his feet slapped upon the interminable paving stones, up the zigzag path, out into the blazing light of the square, past the temple with its yellow-veined columns, hurrying by all the black statues. He was breathless by the time he pushed through the groaning door and into the Palatine's Latin library, where he fell like a lion upon Julius, Julius with his vague eyes and shabby cloak, Julius the library's keeper.

What did he know? What had he heard?

Nothing—

Nothing!

Well, yes, it seemed there was some interest somewhere—but no one knew who, or what.

Ovid stood still, in the large quiet room, all its cabinets stuffed with scrolls and the light slanting down through the dusty air, and imagined himself silently exploding. He thanked Julius and went away again, eyes straining once more toward Augustus's palace portals, and plodded back down the granite path to lie again in his black bedroom and wait.

Finally, at the end of the second week, word came. Carus had just arrived, impatient for Ovid to hear the latest installation in his endless epic—Carus with his long, shapely legs, running his hand through his hair as he asked after Ovid's work but spoke of his own; Carus, most dear and most enraging companion, fellow socialite, bitter rival. They were in the study, Ovid in his lion-clawed chair and Carus pacing, flinging his wrist as he recited, when at the same moment two things happened. In the middle of a windy sentence, Carus fell silent, his opal eyes fixed upon something in the garden—and there was Xenia, lips open in that smile, sun shining through her yellow dress. At that instant, someone rapped on the door—a significant rapping, perfunctory. Ovid and Carus looked at each other through the still air as Persilla hurried to the door, and in came the messenger, with his miraculous summons.

Later, Ovid remembered this visitation as being accompanied by fragrant wings that muffled the ordinary sounds of the day, carrying him off—as Ganymede might have felt when Jove sent down his eagle. Goodbye to Carus, goodbye! Ovid's elegant toes brushed his old friend's pointed, jealous ears, as he was borne aloft, up, up the Palatine . . .

At the dusk of this miraculous day, he stood in the garden with a bowl of wine, his eyes still glazed from what had happened. The sun was setting, the sky a cool violet; the garden had a moist evening smell. There was a quietness in the air, a sense of still satisfaction. Ovid leaned against the granite herm and gazed up. The world about him was finally right: all its colors and forms, from the shimmering palm fronds to a floating cloud, were peaceful, perfectly placed. When Xenia came out, he raised his arm to the sky and toasted it—and realized that she had been right. It had happened, he told her: he'd been taken up, taken in.

"In magnificent feathery wings," he said. He waltzed slowly around the herm, sprinkling wine upon its lascivious face. Oh, god, how he loved that darling work. Echo! Narcissus! Pygmalion! He was rising, rising; he could *feel* himself floating, ever closer to the deified wrinkled heels of Vergil and Horace. This patron, of all patrons!

There had, once upon a time, been such literary circles presided over by women, in the days of the old republic. Dilettantes, probably, but at least they spent their gold properly. And it was fitting that he should be the first poet chosen by this new patroness, in this brand-new empire. He, like a dark moth, would hover around her slender light, the two of them casting far shadows. She was so eager, burning, her eyes all fire! Although she'd whispered, very coy, she preferred that no one know about this arrangement just yet. No, no—of course not, he'd cried. He understood completely! But how he wanted to tell, to take this miraculous Xenia in his arms and swing her over the garden and crow out his marvelous news!

"But who is he?" she asked.

Ovid looked at her, noting her limitations with the same

wonder with which he'd just seen her skill, and marveled at the possibility that presented itself. He paused to take another drink, the bowl in one large cradling hand. Of course, *patron* was hardly the word, but the female form sounded odd—and now the idea glimmered that this imprecision might be useful.

"Well, in fact I can't tell you who, it's a secret just now," he said, fingers drumming his cup.

All that evening, Ovid shielded himself with wine. He'd never liked heavy drinking; his reputation as dissolute was based entirely on his writings, which was a compliment, he supposed. But as the evening went on and he sat with that lovely feline girl on the couch opposite his own, nibbling with her sharp little teeth at slices of gourd (sweetened with honey, spiced with dense fish sauce), he took up his wine, sloshed it about—above all was incoherent—so he could coil himself up inside and think. As soon as she kissed his hot face good night and went off to her room, he put aside the bowl and blew out the lamp so he could ponder, at peace, in the dark.

It was a coup, what had happened today. A stunning coup— he still could not quite believe it. To have left Rome last spring under such tense conditions, and then to have won this particular patron. When he'd arrived in her exquisite little chamber this morning after receiving her summons, she'd smothered him with praise like kisses, and he had stood there modulating his face while he snatched at the fluttering words and stuffed them in his greedy chest to feast upon later.

Then—only moments after that deluge of praise, once she'd settled him on silk chartreuse cushions and offered him roasted flamingo tongues—she pressed on. "Are you working on something *now?*" He was startled, but of course he shouldn't be, he told himself harshly. Of course. There must always be another

project—otherwise, what need of a patron? The momentary
bitterness was swallowed, along with one slender black tongue,
and he nodded, smiled, said nothing definitive. Yet even if he
was still halfway undecided, he couldn't afford to be anymore:
his heart locked around the idea that had been growing since
that night in the forest.

She went on, his patroness, enjoying her new role. "This
next one," she said, "your next work must be—" and here she
struggled for words, her eyes drifting off through the window,
upon the clouds. Her red-jeweled fingers lightly stroked the air,
and she seemed to be fashioning it to her will, having it take on
substance as only people in her position might, those accus-
tomed to having their whims turned solid.

"Your next work must not be so—" and again she stopped,
searching the sky for her meaning. "Not so *promiscuous*," she
said at last, smiling fully upon him.

Promiscuous! His very own word. He was astonished and
felt giddy heat on his brow. Then he realized: what with
promiscuity being his alleged offense, she was offering him a
way to safety, leading him toward the ivory gates—in fact, she
herself was the gatekeeper.

"Something *grave*," she continued, rubbing her hands, her
slim foot jogging, as if she were the one who would grow incandescent with the effort of creating. "Do you have a new subject
yet? Something serious, something *singular*?" And as she again
used his own word and looked at him with her shining dark
eyes, he felt for a panicked moment that she knew, that she
could see the secret inside him.

Ovid had gazed off vaguely toward the clouds at that, his
heart hammering in his ribs. Then he stood up and settled his
shoulders, smiling down, desperate to feel his full height, to

unfold his long form and force upon her the effect it always had on women. And indeed she smiled back, made a show of retreating. She'd accepted that he would not tell her yet; that was his prerogative. But he'd bring a few scraps as they came?

So, he thought now, lying upon the couch in the dark—so it is really beginning. And, if I can believe *her*, this marvelous Xenia, it will be my best.

But should he believe her?

Why not? When she'd known what she had about the *Metamorphoses*!

And if she knew that this next one would be even better, did that mean she knew what it was?

She couldn't. She hadn't known anything about his patroness, after all. Odd, her little blind spots.

He saw then the gold spots on that piece of green silk, the one she'd tied around her mouth. Blind spots, he thought, yes, and large ones.

He felt a tremor inside him and, rolling over, pondered her lit windows, her form moving within. In the past few days he'd watched as she spent whole minutes immobile, her face to the wall—scrutinizing it, apparently. Or hearing one of those things she heard? He'd watched her crouching, as she had on her pebbles, tracing the floor's pattern with her finger, as if she could divine in some artisan's toil with bits of colored stone a cryptic, critical message. Something shriveled hung from one window; she'd nailed that bronze mermaid to her door. She'd set out rows of pots in the atrium, in the impluvium and all around it, vines dangling from the ceiling. He'd watched her striding about the garden, her dress gathered in one hand, commanding Lazar and Lida while the cook's boy, Tibo, hop-scotched over the freshly turned mounds.

Ovid found that he was pressing the nail of his middle finger sharply into his palm, and stopped. He touched his tongue to the salty cut. Then abruptly stood from the couch, flung his hands to his high square hips, and forced his long legs to pace the floor, to etch out his solid place on the earth. He strode into the portico, making his mantle billow and swing, feeling his physical presence grow more definite with each step. He stopped and gazed again through the dark greenery, toward that sequence of windows.

Only one glowed now, faintly, as though the lamp had been lowered, keeping something secret. He peered so intently that he nearly felt himself slip free, glide like a bat over the palm trees and lemons, wing through her window, cling noiseless to her ceiling. At that moment there was a flash of blue, which dissolved as suddenly as it had appeared, leaving a trace of smoke and a phantom imprint in the darkness. The oil lamp was moved, purple shadows cast all over the walls, and when the light settled he saw her take a step back, hands held out in triumph. And then she turned, fully conscious, to where he watched from the shadows. For a moment they stood that way, he in the portico, she in her room, their eyes held together, in collusion.

He exhaled slowly. Well, then. He would get her stocked; he would find her subjects. And, he realized with a little cool flare, he needn't worry anymore about the law. With this fabulous protectoress, he'd be immune; he'd have nothing to fear.

As she washed her face in a bronze bowl of water and watched a bright drop roll down her arm, carrying the reflected lamplight with it, and wondered again if it was *light* that held the quintessence, and, if so, how exactly to capture it, and whether Ovid would make her into someone like Circe, with her entrancing, laughing spells—but no, she'd rather be Orpheus, mesmerizing the underworld—Xenia thought again of what she'd seen earlier in the day. The news of the patron was not a surprise. She'd known the *Metamorphoses* would be celebrated and had hinted as much, although he hadn't believed her. But today, with Carus, she'd seen something else. He was nearly as tall and as elegant as Ovid, and she knew the two had roamed the streets together, been gallants at the same parties, rivaled each other in poetry, exchanged sharp criticisms. She had watched Carus striding back and forth across the floor, in and out of the shadows. His sculpted face, his arrogant hands. She'd watched him shrug off something Ovid said, saw him laugh dryly, run a hand through his hair. Yet—though he posed and threw back his head in laughter; though his ambition burned ulcerous right through his cool surface; though, when Ovid looked away, Carus fixed him with a look of hungering envy—all the time, as he recited, dust was falling silently upon him. Soft gray dust, sifting from the sky. It settled upon his cropped dark hair, upon his lashes and the bone of his nose, upon his confident, purple-mantled shoulders. It settled upon his leather boots and clung to his arms and his long, shapely hands; it buried his knees and his thighs, and fixed him there, rising slowly up to his chest. As she stood in the garden, she saw him disappear. Not a word Carus wrote would be remembered.

But Ovid. All that time, watching his friend, he was untouched, immaculate. If anything, he gleamed even brighter. His lucid head, his mobile hands—Ovid shone like mercury.

4

They went plunging into the city, Ovid tall, the Roman sun copper upon his lean face, Xenia flying wild at his side. Down the granite road and into the great square with its starkness and majesty, all columns and drapery and intoning men—a blinding dazzle, with brilliantly painted sculptures, all the dark faces and eyes. Then through colonnades, porticoes, more rows of statues, over Augustus's polished plaza, under a huge arch, and into the Subura. The streets here were narrow and steep, choked with vendors selling bread, chickens and game birds, olives, honey, oil, peas, radishes, artichokes, figs, grapes, quinces, dates, fish still flapping, sausages, dormice. And everywhere was the salty smell that came from the pots of garum, tiny fish stewing in melting salt in the sun.

Such a mass of food, such a mass of people! Ovid watched as she drank it all up, her eyes bright with excitement, her small teeth visible between her lips. She'd never seen so many people, he realized, and if it was true that she could *hear* what they thought . . . Africans, tall Hibernians, Greeks selling books, beaky Gauls, black-haired Asians, Egyptians, Syrians, Thracians, Pannonians, Jews, Arabs, Goths—all the peoples of the empire, all their languages, all their different costumes and smells. Slaves, or freedmen, or citizens of Rome and its provinces: one knew by what they wore. But amid all this her foreignness stood out: eyes trailed after her as she passed, mouths hung open at the sight of her eyes.

They went over to the Campus Martius, where the good shops sold exquisite carved furniture, sculptures, bolts of cloth. Xenia gazed entranced through open doors at glimpses of rich atriums, glowing gardens, elegant lunching figures; she stared at groups of young men, arm in arm, proud with their shapely cheekbones and oiled hair, moving through the streets with sidelong looks at the women. And such women, rustling by, with their confectionary hair and quick mouths, their skillfully outlined eyes, the touches of slate blueing their foreheads, the colored jewels upon their arms.

Ovid's book was in the windows, displayed in all the stalls of the Greeks, with a cerulean slipcover setting off the gold bosses. Men and women stood reading it, lips moving, absorbed, lost in the clever nets of his words. And when he passed like a fleeting shadow, fingers touched papyrus anew.

Then how eyes ran all over them, over Ovid and his fabulous consort! His name was whispered; it flew in thrilled cries up over the heads, into the glorious sunlight.

"Ovid, Ovid! Welcome back!"

"God, how Rome's missed you!"

"The book's brilliant, just brilliant!"

"Stunning—a triumph!"

And all the kisses, and the moist frantic eyes, and the nudging of patriarchal elbows, and the gazes full of wonder at his depths, and the longing looks of the younger poets, and the subtle seductive smiles of the women . . .

Ah, little book, darling little book! He clasped Xenia's waist tightly and bit her on the neck.

Who on earth is she? He could hear it, he swore, the hurried whisper. And if *he* could hear it, imagine what *she* heard! Beside him she was inflamed, those fantastic eyes positively glowing, a flush on her snowy chest. Suddenly he flew out of himself, swooped alongside like Vergil's Rumor, and saw the stunning pair of them: all his angular darkness, Xenia's brilliant, strange beauty. *Flamboyant!* he thought—and saw the pure blue flame, the two of them floating finer than air. No: he stopped abruptly in the street to alter the image. No, she was the moon, all light and blue shadow, and he, wicked and knowledgeable in his dark cloak (forbidden—no matter, now!), had pulled her down from the sky, as any sorcerer could. Yes, *he* was the sorcerer, she was the moon. He had Paelignian blood, didn't he? Paelignians, famed for their witchcraft!

"Did you know that?" he asked, and began to tell, but she looked as if she couldn't hear, and he suddenly felt foolish.

"I'm sorry," she said. "It's so loud. The buildings—"

"Yes?"

She shrugged. "They keep falling."

He looked around, askance, and then again at her, at the sunlight passing through the lens of her gold eye, and felt the slightest stab.

She bought oil lamps wrought like faces, their caroling mouths issuing flame, and a bronze stove with a fish as its spout and small birds crowning the lid. She bought skeins of silk, much too precious to do anything with, which she crumpled in her hand, her eyes shut in pained pleasure. He stood back as she plunged into the shops, flushed with desire, and staggered, laden, out.

At the top of the Subura they followed a street that was so steep it became a staircase, until they reached the door they'd sought, opened only after three sharp knocks. There Xenia found a few of the things she wanted, but she was appalled at how few, and at how expensive they were.

"What do you want with carpet bugle?" a woman with a face like a frog whispered, peering out from the dark doorway. Ovid glanced at Xenia, but she flushed, defiant, and held out her hand for the stuff. They gave the woman her money and ran.

Ah, he could feel her excitement, how it was heated by the faintest fear.

Soon she had begun her work, all within perfect view of his study, all carefully monitored by him. She placed rows of jars along her windows, jars of sea-green glass, or clear amethyst, or glowing dandelion yellow. Xenia sat Persilla before her in a chair by the window, where the tiny old woman—her feet not touching the ground—folded her hands together and allowed herself to be examined. Lazar's eyes strained like a horse's as he saw Xenia's fingertips draw near his pocked skin. And Lida: soon Xenia was modeling wax dolls and burning fragments of cloth and hair, her voice and the girl's low in the dark garden; Lida even had a few of her love's fingernails, torn with his teeth and left behind in her bed. Ovid watched all this like a patron, from his thronelike seat that looked into the garden.

Other clients came—just slaves, he'd decided; best to be a little hush-hush. A friend of Lida's, who badly wanted a dream sent to a particular man; Lazar's old aunt, who was set on a curse. They crept around the portico, glancing nervously at the witnessing herm. When they saw Xenia's eyes, flight ran visibly through them, but she caught them and pulled them in and sat them down and began. Usually it was clear at once what was needed, she proclaimed: she could see the problem hovering. That added to the effect, when she knew before they dared open their brown-toothed mouths just what it was that haunted them.

Only once did she seem to flounder: when Ovid was out, a young woman came, Xenia told him, bundled against the autumn rain, the hood of her mantle letting drops fall upon her slender long nose. About her Xenia saw only darkness, everything but her hands, and from them came a hot reddish glow. Xenia assumed that a curse was wanted and drew out a lead tablet. But no: the woman, her eyes sliding in and out of Xenia like needles, had wanted something simple, ilex drops for a baby.

He could see how Xenia thrilled, how she saw herself anew: here in Rome, with her brilliance and daring, with *him*, gazed upon and adored. He could see her hold herself carefully, posing as she imagined his subject should be. Now he had begun in earnest at last; his best work had set sail, his stylus cleaving the smooth black wax with line after subtle line. He read them off hoarsely to his patroness and stood straight as a mast to receive her praise. In the streets, in the baths, in the shops, he was greeted like a visiting deity. How he'd surprised them! What depths he'd shown! He felt it as he walked his beloved city, himself made of some ancient material, of earth and marble and warmed red brick, himself becoming eternal.

So she was flush, and he was flush, and three weeks after the book appeared on the streets—three weeks after Ovid himself appeared with that far-flung beauty—Marcus threw one of his famous parties to celebrate the *Metamorphoses*.

There were nine couches, enough for twenty-seven guests, arranged in a pattern requiring great agility of the slaves. Ovid, of course, would sit at the top corner, next to Marcus, with Xenia over and down, beside Carus. She wore apricot silk, and with that luminous hair dressed in silver and seashells, and that delicate skin twined with silver as well—there was a silence when they entered, a slow outlet of breath. Then her name raced around the great room, and Ovid felt, to his astonishment, a sudden desire to seize her and cloak her, a pang lest things slip from his hands.

He stayed as close as he could: she was excited but visibly stunned, seeing and hearing, as she no doubt did, the mirrors and echoes of things. But almost at once she was taken from him, caught up in fascinated female hands and led away by them, and Carus. Ovid himself could barely see through all the fluttering lilac and rose that flocked about him, settling upon him like doves. A new beauty he'd never met (but of course he couldn't know *all* of them), a creature in transparent lacewing green, with gold all over her arms and a lissome back and deadly violet eyes, was seated beside him and praised his book in such gratifying detail—the sort of praise he never got enough of, when the intelligence beneath his seemingly airiest lines was divined and clasped to a breast. And what a fine breast . . .

Falernian wine, Caecuban, Massic—Marcus brought out the silver flagons with tiny scenes worked in. The wines, Ovid thought as he drank toast after toast, were rich with Horace; he'd made their names mythic—more than mythic, enduring. Yet it was *he*, Ovid, being toasted tonight! His praises rang all around, passages from the *Metamorphoses* were recited and shivered over in glee.

"Philomela's tongue—horrific!" croaked Marcus.

"Oh, but confess it, so very funny!"

"And the plangency of Arethusa melting into water . . ."

"The brilliance of the Narcissus doublets!"

"That terrible longing of Myrrha for her father . . ."

"So wonderfully perverse," murmured Julius.

"But so *sickly* convincing!" cried the lacewing.

Yes, it was true, it was all true; Ovid suddenly could not believe he had created them, those darlings. He found that he was close to tears. Dear Marcus!—he toasted dear Marcus. And Julius—Julius too, keeper of that most precious library, where the works of Ovid had their own private niche! And Celus, and Bassus, and, good god, Atticus, and even jealous Carus! And this lacewing here, so lively, so bright, why not toast her, too! Up rose his cup, up rose her cup, her throat that muscled type he so liked . . .

"But tell us," someone said, "what now?"

What now? He swallowed. He would not answer *that*.

"All right, then, tell us about this new patron."

"Yes, you tormented us before. Now tell!"

Tell. He nearly did, in his enthusiasm; it was burning in his jubilant mouth. But of course he was not to tell; he'd promised—and suddenly he wondered why. The interlocking tables, the undulating floor, the walls flickering with stories, the food whirling by on the hands of slaves with all the names cried out—oysters from Circeo and Baian cockles and livers of flounder and African snails—and this sheer green woman here beside him, so wonderfully ripe, the warmth of her rounded arm at his thigh: he never drank this much, never . . . Suddenly he remembered Xenia. He clapped for water, smiling, anxious, and shook his head at his friends.

She was ringed by Carus and a trio of old beauties he knew: Celia, with hennaed hair; Flavia, with blondined ringlets; and a dark one, Egyptian, whose name he forgot but the smell of whose armpits still lived in his mind. Xenia was drinking wine much too quickly, as their chatter darted about her like fire.

"I was Corinna, as I expect he told you."

"Ridiculous! *I* was."

"Oh, please!"

"I'd say you need a new one," whispered the lacewing beside him. "Someone not quite so antique."

"—crane roasted in salt and surrounded by blackbirds—"

Xenia was stiff, she did not look right, and he wondered then if she saw pasts as well. He felt sick, suddenly seeing all those sloppy lost moments . . .

"Ah, the famous Corinna, and then—what was her name?"

"Can't remember, she didn't last."

"But after *her*—"

"Well—"

At that, the wicked trio looked at each other, those dark eyes flying from one to the other like torches, and laughed, and the way Xenia eyed them and then stared into her wine cup, he thought, Yes, horrible, she sees it all. He cleared his throat to intervene, but this lacewing—

"I know, you know, what that meant," she murmured, "about Philomela's tongue. Cut out, but still alive." She sighed and leaned closer, her dress falling open (as intended), so he (as intended) looked. "You meant your tongue, your words, living on. You see," she whispered, "I know you." She smiled. But beyond her gold-twined arm he saw Xenia's face, and he thought with a jolt, She heard.

The lacewing followed his gaze, and he saw how her violet eyes found Xenia, weighed her, dismissed her—and how Xenia saw this as well.

"You know all about him, of course, don't you, Xenia?"

Those Harpies, clamoring, he could see them tear flesh! Now this creature placed her hand on his arm.

"There's something," she whispered, "I'd just love to show you."

"—the sauce made of Venafrum oil and chopped herbs—"

"Darling Ovid." The Egyptian. "He just can't be trusted."

"God, no. But loved . . ."

"—Alban grapes dried in smoke with wild Umbrian boar—"

Xenia's eyes were fixed upon the woman beside him, those slanting yellow-and-gray eyes. Oh, god, he thought, does she *see* something?

"It's just in the garden, if you'll come . . ."

"It always seemed so strange of Ovid," Flavia was saying, "to have made that little arrangement years ago."

"Well, it was logical, given the law. Better that than have to pay the bachelor fines."

"So expensive not to be married!"

"Not to mention having no children."

"And what could have been more convenient—a widow with a child who needed the arrangement as much as he did!"

"And wanted as little to do with him as he with her!"

"But still—"

"To have given up on love altogether!"

"*Love*, perhaps . . ."

"But not lovers!"

The lacewing stood, touching his hand, and Xenia—he saw something shoot through her body.

"Will you come?"

And he could not help it, he had to see how it would play. So
he felt himself rise behind that shapely green hip, he felt himself move through the interlocking couches, he felt himself pass
before Xenia's hot eyes. But there he paused, uncertain. Awk-
wardly he looked at her, knowing his eyes were muddied, his
knowing only making it worse. He—of all people—did not
know what to do. So he nearly smiled, and didn't quite, and
touched her cheek with a cold hand. Then turned in disarray
and went out to the garden, to that woman waiting in the dark.

It was black, that was all, everything was black. All but her
white, staring eyes. Xenia knew this was disproportionate,
laughable, but there was absolutely nothing she could do.

That touch: something in her seemed to know it. Goodbye.

The women were looking at her with all their eyes and their
breathing dark lips, full of sympathy and hot pleasure. They
glanced at Ovid's empty place, and at the lacewing's abandoned
cup, and at the shadows close in the garden. She did not know
what to do. The blackness seemed to envelop her, smoking.
Treacherous. She looked down, as if she might see herself disappear, because that's what she was doing. She lifted her cup and
shut her eyes at the trembling liquid, smelling the cold, wet silver, and drank. She sensed a shaking of women's heads.

"What were we saying? Ah, yes: *lovers.*"

"But look at us, we're speaking as if Xenia weren't even
here."

"Which you are, now, aren't you?"

"You've come a long way."

"—the caviar is in wine lees, the grapes with Picenum
apples—"

Xenia felt as if her body were smoking. She drank again to cool herself but grew only hotter.

"Did you really live at the end of the world?" one of the women began brightly. "That's what Carus says, don't you, Carissimus?"

"—how clever, black salt and white pepper! Did you notice? I didn't until I tasted—"

She would not look in the garden, not see those shadows so close.

"People really *live* in the Caucasus?"

"Impressive you speak any Latin at all, coming from way up there."

"But is it up? Or over? I can't quite see it . . ."

This heat, she could barely breathe; the air was stifling and dense. Then she realized—there was smoke; there was fire. She clutched the couch. There were flames, here on the Esquiline, a conflagration that would rage from the circus and run wild through tenements and houses until half the city was engulfed. This house would burn: she saw it now, the flames in the atrium, the garden lit red.

The women clucked and pursed, their eyes on her as she stared through them.

"But do they really have fish legs?" one asked nervously.

"I've heard they eat babies!"

"And is the place full of witches?"

The flames flew from the atrium door, and the dry palm trees caught fire at once with a crackle, the marble benches splitting in the heat. She could almost feel it on her face as the flames rushed toward the dining-room door—where Ovid now appeared.

"There are some," Xenia heard herself say as he passed, all the women's eyes following.

"Really, witches! How exciting."

Now *she* came in—his new Corinna. And suddenly Xenia saw: *she* would be there when the fire ravaged Rome. Yet so old, that delectable flesh like tangled string on her bones, the only light in her eyes the reflected flames as she ran frantically from room to room.

"So are you a witch?" asked Carus. "Have you enthralled him?"

But someone laughed a nasty laugh, and it was *she*, oblivious and young. "Ovid enthralled? Does he *look* it?" She smiled and smoothed her dress.

The women grew watchful. Carus leaned forward. Xenia gazed through the green dress at the flames licking the frame of the dining-room door.

"But that doesn't make her not a witch," said the lacewing. "Just an ineffective one. If you're really a witch, tell me my fortune. Isn't that what they do? Glass bowls and all? Here, here's a cup."

"Oh, now," murmured Celia, and Flavia frowned, as the woman thrust out a cup of wine and the fire tumbled into the room.

"So what do you see?"

The lacewing shook the cup in her hand, but now the flames were a pace away, the gold paint blistering from a wall, its images blackening, bits of stucco beginning to fall.

"Or do you need special contraptions?"

The flames were licking the mosaic black as they raced over the floor toward this woman—but so old, standing there fixed in terror, the fire darting in her eyes.

"You see," she said. "She sees nothing."

She turned the cup over, the wine splashing—and at that

the flames leapt up, snatched at her dress, flew through her hair. And Xenia said just what she saw.

Ovid looked up then; everyone did. The women were staring, the lacewing staggering sick from the room, but Xenia herself, glowing cold, was fixing a shell in her hair.

As the party broke up moments later, Carus pulled Ovid aside. "Whoever your patron is, you know, you might be a little more careful."

5

After that night it was quiet, a quiet that fit the cool, bright days, still and removed. No one came to the house. Marcus gave Ovid a wide berth, merely flashing at him with his eyebrows on the street. And Julius, Julius was always so abstracted. Ovid saw only Carus, occasionally, at the baths. There was a chill, and Ovid decided now that he found it salutary: the cold plunge after the sweat bath. He didn't mind if no one came; they'd always come around later. He was ready to work—he had a store of material.

Extraordinary—to find she was so *flammable*—when all he'd done was gone and listened to some appalling verse. Xenia had been ice-hot, her eyes glassy as he'd smuggled her home. He'd been afraid to speak of what she'd actually seen and said, waiting until the next day. Yet when he questioned her, gingerly, she didn't even seem altogether to remember her little slip. As if something had leapt from her mouth, something had leapt from her *soul* . . .

He wrote that down now, the thought settling into a flowing line, like a bird landing on water. *Her flesh*, she'd said simply, *burned away from her bones, all that bloody steam.*

He shuddered. Could she really *see* that? He looked down at his own arm and felt again the pall that had fallen upon the room. *You might be a little more careful* . . .

Of course, Carus couldn't really know anything. He was a peacock. Officious. And dull—that moldering epic Ovid had promised to get through! He drew a peacock with a fan of ornate, curlicue feathers, admired it sidewise in the sun, and then thought of Io guarded by peacock-Argus, once she'd been seduced by Zeus . . .

He wished Carus had not sat beside Xenia. A mistake: he should have sat by her himself. He felt hot all at once, his wrists slick and sticking, and erased the peacock he'd drawn.

Whoever your patron is . . . He shifted in his chair, put his stylus aside, again irked by the strictures of secrecy. No, it was sensible, logical. A trial period, given his reputation. What else could he possibly expect?

An interview, he thought without meaning to. He blinked the thought away. No, no interview. What, with *him*? Augustus? Outrageous, much too early.

The oleander stirred in the warm winter sun. The cook's boy, Tibo, was lying spread-eagled on the pebbles, fanning his arms and legs to make a butterfly—or, given that shaved black head, a bat. From the herm's long shadow, the orange cat watched. Tibo's eyes rolled slowly toward it, and idly he wiggled one finger; the cat closed its eyes at him, and licked.

Her jealousy, Ovid thought: it was not the ordinary sort, even for a first outbreak. He knew jealousy, and the Roman variety he knew so well mostly burned the skin. Cause for theatrics, but there was too much insulation here, too much distraction; it was a part of the city and had its place. Like the Furies—who had once dwelled deep in the earth, emerging to

make parents devour their own children and make children
murder their parents, but who more recently had been dredged
up and civilized, offered uniforms and weapons, enlisted in the
service of the state.

Xenia's jealousy was not civilized. It lurked like those more
ancient Furies, somewhere inside her, like that whiff of cold rot
from deep in the ground that had infused her the night he'd
spied on her. And at the slightest betrayal it would be a fearful
thing, violent and immolating.

So he'd sworn to her as they clattered home—and he'd
meant it, the whole thing was so alarming—that he'd done
nothing, he was impervious to that green girl's ordinary
charms. He was so alarmed that he swore, on things he did hold
dear, that he wouldn't, he would never, come near another
woman. He trembled, even, saying it.

Yet all the while he could see the potential. As if there were
two of him: poet and man.

But when he'd sworn all those things—the peace it brought
her! Astonishing, a milky peace, so that she was like a com-
forted child safe enough to sleep. He had felt—yes—so
relieved. He'd smiled and touched her hot eyelids, felt himself
melting with tenderness, and carried her liquid, dreaming body
over the garden and into bed.

The dreaming body that he daily plundered.

He gazed now into the glowing garden, at the feathered
shadows made by the palms, at the little boy, whose dark eyes
were pondering him as if they could see into his heart, and Ovid
felt a slight fissuring. He looked down at his tablet, his hand.
He rubbed his eyes, rubbed his lips, and shook his head.

For there she was, stepping into her workroom. She was
drenched in sun, with her slender luminous arms and proud

high chin, her hair blazing around her. Her eyes went slowly to him and, reaching his, lingered in that gaze like welding gold.

Circe, he thought. Daughter of the sun. How could *he* plunder *her*?

It was all alchemy now, her forehead furrowed, quick fingers measuring as she bent over her alembic. She had declared that she was bored with futures and dreams; she'd done them a thousand times. Now she would do what she was determined to do: find the *quinta essentia*. The bright mercury danced in the egg-shaped glass—

Mercury, *egg*: very useful! Words with so much play to them. The very sight of her, and his black wax tablets began to fill, his eyes unblinking, hectic. If a word jarred it was violently struck out, a neat peel of wax on the tip of his stylus flicked off with his thumb. She worked, he watched, she watched him watch, and his imagination flew. She seemed to warm beneath his fevered hand, to melt, to flow, to turn to waxen words.

At last he looked up, hollowed, exhausted. The sun had lowered, the light grown cool. Xenia put down a glass vial, and her eyes traveled toward his. Then he watched as, her eyes fixed upon him, she came gliding through the portico, her body, pale blue-veined marble like the columns, moving in and out of the shadows. Soundlessly she entered the study. She crept behind his chair and traced her fingertips behind his ears; she ran her cool tongue over his hot lids, brushing his neck with the tips of her breasts. A bird was calling in the garden, an early-evening call, sweet and clear; the palm fronds rustled gently. She moved around him, and her fingers slipped into his clothes at his shoulder, and glided in teasing patterns down over his chest, the delicate folds of his stomach, toward the tense hollow of his hip. Into his curls, along his silky little limb, her touch like cool lightning. With her soft wet kisses she followed her fingers, lighting the zones of his body one by one, until all his consciousness had sunk and he'd swollen, the garden swimming before his eyes, his mouth flooded with desire, and it was she in the chair, she had transformed him, and he was on his knees, his teeth sinking into her skin. As his hands devoured her white thighs and his tongue slipped in between, he marveled again at how she melted, how she seemed to turn to liquid glass, and he thought, as he sank at last inside her and under the depths of the sea, that it was miraculous, miraculous, to have such a Galatea, who willed herself reckless into art.

On a sunny winter day, wisps of smoke rising from the baked brown city, Ovid strode home through the cypresses along the granite path. His patroness's slim foot had jogged as he read to her, her dark eyes glowing and her breath quick: she was pleased. He had felt the warmth of her pleasure as he left her, as he passed through the dark hall and dim atrium, all the way out of the compound. Then why did he now feel so empty, so drained?

It must be this new life, he decided as he reached his front door. Reclusiveness did not come naturally to him. No parties, no long nights stretched out in dining rooms, surrounded by clever chatter, lovely bare arms, competition. No stimulating trips to the theater or the circus; he was even cautious about roaming the bookstalls of the Greeks. He glimpsed people he knew in the porticoes but turned quickly away, pretending to be distracted. The isolation parched him. Beauty needs oiling, needs polishing, he'd once written, advising girls to take lovers. But so, it seemed, did he: without polish, he creaked; his tongue went dry in his mouth. Each time he saw Carus (god, he still hadn't read that wretched epic), he found himself glib and deflecting, while Carus scrutinized him with his opal eyes.

Still, parched or not, the past several weeks had been hugely productive. He'd finished the first three acts, watching Xenia through the study window late into the night while she bent over her own work, isolating elements, altering them through mercuric heat, determined to make pure light. She had dozens of dead insects in a jar, gathered for her by an excited Tibo, who was always poised in corners or monkeyed up trees, eyes intent and grubby hand ready. She let him watch as she subjected the dead mosquitoes and beetles to vapors, heat, and rays of light. Oh, she would force the world to her will, she would break the dire rule of nature! Ovid wondered what she thought of her own transformation, her slim white belly growing so round, her fingers and feet so plump that she looked as if she'd sprung someone else's. He saw her sometimes gazing at them, holding her hands to the light of the oil flame.

Ovid passed through the atrium with its damp smell of soil, his skin feeling loose upon his ostrich bones. Trailing a hand through some lily-like leaves, he paused, closed his eyes, and acknowledged that what he felt was the first hint of that empty spiraling . . . The material had been pouring out of him, more quickly, more violently, than any ever had, so that he was stunned each time he emerged from the trance of work and looked down to see what he had written. Day after day he had charged up the Palatine, paced, read, and then stood calmly by the window as his patroness's praise showered upon him like gold—and as she urged him relentlessly on. On and on. He felt driven, exhausted. After weeks of this, he could feel himself running dry.

He went to his study and dropped his work upon the table, the tablets loose, the rolls of polished text unfurling from their carelessly tied ribbons. That was all, he thought, gazing at his own lines. There was nothing else yet, nothing in his mind; he could not begin the fourth act. Time was what he most needed, he told himself quickly—but it was more than that: he needed more substance, more *complexity*. Yet what this would be, and how to form it, he simply could not see. He sat down, one arm stretched out, and looked at Xenia across the garden. No: he had scraped up all he could, and though he stared at her, though he stared at his tablets, he could see nothing more.

Xenia was sitting with her dried roots and unguents, lackadaisically grinding powders. He watched her hand circle slowly, watched the rise and fall of her shoulders. Abruptly, she stopped. She held the egg-shaped pestle in her open palm, stared dully at it, then let it drop.

Sirocco, he thought. She was growing bored. She might fly.

Across the garden, Xenia was drawing listless circles on her chart, which had barely altered during all these months in Rome, despite the addition of a few new colors. She put down her pen and gazed over at Ovid, who sat staring up at the sky. She bent her strength on seeing into his mind, seeing what was there, what she was to *do*—because surely something must happen. Was she to be Circe, turning men into pigs? Orpheus, making rocks sing? Or Psyche herself, voyaging for love to the underworld and miraculously finding her way out again?

She saw nothing, just his lean dark head, his lifeless eyes. The air was heavy and still.

He was rolling his pen back and forth on the table; she could almost hear him breathe. He looked up but did not meet her eyes. In the garden, the lemon leaves rustled; a speck of ash drifted upon the herm. She drew another slow circle on her chart and became aware of her heart thudding in her ribs. She found herself counting its beats as a bare, dry emptiness opened up inside her, and she thought, He is growing bored, he will fly.

It was nearly an hour later—when the light had drained from the sky, when Ovid had felt himself begin to spiral away, when Xenia's heartbeats had become so loud that she almost could not breathe—that there was a sudden brisk tapping upon Ovid's screen. He looked at once through the dusky garden at Xenia; she looked through it at him. Then Persilla appeared in his study, spoke to him in a quick, low voice, and within seconds the air was electric. For it seemed that the cook's boy was possessed by something fantastic, more than an illness, something protean and unconquerable—Xenia's task, at last.

6

Drusa, the cook, had green rings of worry around her eyes when Xenia hurried up to the slaves' rooms. Tibo was limp, his cheeks and forehead burning—symptoms that were common enough. But in his room hung an underground vapor that troubled her, and around his coughing mouth hovered a ghostly white ring—she had never seen anything like it—as if it were the trace of what had plunged into his body, like a ring of bubbles left on the sea. She felt Ovid's eyes upon her as she examined the boy, as she consulted her chart and made her lists, as she gathered her things to go out.

The morning was foggy, with a burning sweetness in the damp air, and the trunks of the cypresses and umbrella pines lining the road were soft and fleshy, their fine needles sheened with moisture. *Control all the subtle things*, she thought as she hurried by. *Penetrate every solid.* An infusion of betony, a goosegrass chaplet, an ivy tincture for his cough, and she'd burn coltsfoot, too, on a cypress coal beside his bed. If there was no betony or goosegrass, there was always periwinkle. And she needed more jars; she must gather Tibo's breath and that of cer-

tain plants. The air that glowed around plants, she'd been
thinking: perhaps the quintessence was there, in that subtle
fusion of light and life . . . She felt flushed and nervous as she
skidded down the damp path, the cold seeping up through her
boots. She must cross the great square, pass under the arch, and
find that narrow street—there weren't so many, were there?
She imagined herself as Alcestis ransoming her husband from
death, or as Psyche throwing drugged cakes to Cerberus so that
she could enter the underworld, or Circe turning the animals
back into men, or Daedalus actually flying. To break the laws of
nature, she thought—so much *more* than the laws of men. By
the time she entered the huge square with all its courts, the saffron veil seemed to billow from her shoulders.

When she began to cross over to the Subura, there was
shouting, and the whole crowd crushed together so that she was
kept to one side of the road. Dark figures emerged from the fog,
crying out and forcing a path. It was *he*, people whispered: the
emperor. His health was terrible, his legs stiffened as if with rust
in the winter. Ovid had told her that in his spartan compound on
the Palatine he slept in the same room summer and winter—
unheard of; the rich spent winter in a room piped with heating.
But Augustus was drear, ostentatiously modest, looking out bale-
fully on those who did not live as he lived, who did not bare
their breasts to the mythic Roman austerity. Even his granddaughter Julia had seen her luxurious summer villa razed.

Xenia pushed her way to the plinth of a temple so she could
see, and there were the African guards, dressed in red and perspiring in the cold air as they shouted and held back the crowd.
Then he appeared, Augustus himself, elbowing away help, his
glaring eyes shooting into the mob. His guards preceded and
followed him but did not walk at his side, as he was not one to

shield himself or fear. Rather, he'd defy the crowd to do to him
as had been done to Caesar; Augustus's darting glances seemed
the avenging ghosts of those senators' famous daggers. His face
was ashen as he slowly, painfully advanced, his eyes cased in
papery skin. It was a punitive face, the face of an old man scraping the earth for the last of what it owed him. But strangely like
Ovid's, Xenia thought suddenly, with that beakish nose, those
hungry eyes—only calcified, where Ovid was all liquid. About
Augustus was the dullness of stone—his image of permanence
being pure stone, he was gradually entombed in it, only his eyes
left mobile.

As she stood there, on a plinth, his eyes came upon her. He
looked at her, and she looked at him, and for one sheer moment
she felt her veil stripped away. Then he passed, this white
specter and his slaves, and behind him life returned, the crowd
once more fluid. She wrapped her mantle close about her and
crossed the square, passing under the huge arch and into the
streets of the Subura.

Raw chickens, goats, the heads of lambs—she was shivering, but here, at least, was the right crossing; she recognized the
carved lantern. There was such a pummeling in her ribs as she
followed the narrow street and climbed at last the dank stairs
that she heard herself gasping in the smoky, sweet air.

The right door: Ovid had reminded her, the one with the
high grated window. Now the triple knock, and she waited,
breathing on her swollen cold hands. She looked up the street,
and down, where it turned a corner into darkness. After a
minute the door opened, the woman peering out as if from a
bristling forest.

"Wood betony," Xenia said quickly. "Goosegrass, britan-
nica." The woman disappeared, returning with packets.

"And peony."

"Peony?" The voice was low.

"Picked at midnight."

She shook her head. "No peony."

"Apollinaris, then." That would do for the pain, either a decoction of the leaves or the oil poured into his ears.

But the woman was not even looking for it; instead, her eyes darted behind Xenia. Thrusting out her packets, she shook her palm for the money, so Xenia slapped down the coins and hurried away down the narrow dank street.

After a few steps she looked over her shoulder. Was there something, silvery, quick?

No. It was a foggy morning, the wet streets full of furtive cats. She hurried on, reciting recipes, conscious of being alone, and pulled her hood around her face to hide her glassy hair. While the betony was boiling she'd twine the stems of those starlike whorls of goosegrass. She had a sliver of dried yellow coltsfoot to place on a chunk of coal and burn by his bed. She could nearly smell it now, that sleepy scent that curled into the nostrils . . .

No—that's not what she smelled. She stopped. That's not what she smelled at all. There was something sickly sweet in the air; she'd been smelling it all morning. What, from the gutters? It was much too refined. It seemed to trail along with her, sickening, her stomach jolting with each step. She bent over suddenly and retched, then hurried away, wiping her mouth. It was like panthers, wild and husky, an animal smell, sweated excitedly from fur. Even the thought of it made her insides squirm again, and she put her hands to her stomach to still it.

But at that moment, her hands feeling the warmth of that small globe, she realized, as if for the first time: here was a *baby*, a little live thing, *Ovid's* baby and *hers*. What a shock! She was flooded with heat, a terrible love that dissolved her.

The world about her seemed suddenly different, clearer and more still. All at once she did not feel alone but invisibly accompanied, both holding and held, so peculiar. It was almost embarrassing, a hot little secret of extraordinary value, and the color came to her cheeks. I can just *think*, she thought, and it will hear.

She gathered her packets, straightened her hood, and went on, altered, as if part of her mind had slipped into a bright new room, and she compelled herself after a moment to attend, or she'd get lost. She'd turned into a street of leatherworkers, with satchels, shoes, skins hanging from hooks. Rabbits, cows, goats, sheep: she glanced at the shapes, the tufts of fur, the awkward dangling hooves. Her eye fell upon a perfect sheepskin, smooth and waxy white inside, with the faintest lacework of veins, the wool soft and cloudy along the edges. But as she looked at it the shimmers began . . . The traces of veins became figured, turned to words, tiny pictures in pure, bright colors: a miniature girl gazing at her hand as it became a claw, a boy turning into a stag, acanthus leaves and ivy twisting all around. So intricate, so lovingly painted! And the hands that painted them—she saw them now. A man's rough hands, reddened with cold, a callus on one thumb, his wrists disappearing into brown wool sleeves. She could hear wax sputter and drip, there was a smell of incense and an unfamiliar light. And the words that were being copied with such care, the letters fashioned like pointed windows, with tiny flanges and wings: *I'll write about bodies transfigured . . .*

Xenia stopped, there in the slippery road, between stalls of swinging hides. *His* words. His gleaming head, his mercurial hand: she saw now what this meant. Ovid was not just the most celebrated poet of his era; he would be read for centuries.

She stood on the wet stones, swaying. Imagine, being read for centuries, by wholly different peoples, in places that don't yet exist. And if *he* would be read for centuries, then *she*—

She skidded, half flying, down the narrow street, through the arch beside Augustus's huge temple, and out into the plaza, stunned, full of this fabulous future. And—*mirabile!*—there was Ovid, in the crowd, the back of his dark sculpted head conspicuous above all the others, his cloak that always billowed. Her new knowledge was shrieking against her teeth as she pushed through people to reach him.

Again there was a jostling, a shoving, and the crowd tightened to make way for a golden box gliding near. Delicately wrought, flashing with color, it hovered like a dragonfly, all eyes upon it. But Ovid alone seemed to see inside the box, through its silken curtains, and he smiled as if upon a secret pleasure. The box stopped and was lowered. The curtain was quickly drawn open by a slender, jeweled hand, and Xenia watched as Ovid stepped from the crowd, took that hand, and slipped in.

7

Ovid was amazed at the fortuitousness of the event—something altogether unplanned, something he'd never have thought of devising. Yet how convenient, how poetically perfect. No sooner had Xenia marched off on what she imagined was her mission than the next phase began on its own: for he'd had no idea she was there in the thronging square, until the litter was lifted and, before the silk curtain was quickly drawn, he saw her framed white face.

When he returned that evening, his nose still cold, he could see it all over her the instant she came into the dining room, yet she said nothing. Those eyes—they were hard and glassy, far. Again she was icy-hot. It made him nervous, lying on his couch, plucking at his roasted quail and raisins. He fingered a wing and faltered a moment, wondering if she could really suffer so for *him.*

But, he reminded himself, he'd done nothing.

A wordless dinner. His eyes moved over her gingerly, waiting, and roved over the painted walls. Good for silences, those walls; all the stories were distracting. He hummed.

At last, after toying awhile with her mouth, she spoke. But what finally came out was an elaborately circuitous remark that bore deep within it, like a jar in a current, a device meant to capture what she wanted: whether he traveled in litters often and, if so, with whom?

There was a silence, in which the air in the red dining room seemed to alter, as if the painted walls had stepped back, casting upon her an interested eye. He regarded her, his lips parted in the driest hint of a smile, and felt the lines of his forehead rise in waves over his bemused eyes, as he stepped into that old, familiar part.

"Do I travel in litters," he said. "Not nearly enough. But you know how I like walking." Oh, so clever. He could see how she bit her tongue not to take the question further.

"Still, sometimes..." He took a mouthful of quail. He looked up at her. "Do you like it?"

"Like what?"

He gestured. "The quail. The sauce, I mean. I've stolen it from Marcus."

She nodded, and put down her plate, and looked with that look through the wall.

"Marcus, for instance," he went on. She turned. "He often uses a litter. But then Marcus, you know, he's so fat."

Too cruel! She could not have seen much—it had been too fast, too dim—but no doubt she had seen something. And no part of Marcus could ever hope to be the slim olive hand that had drawn shut that curtain.

"Of course," he said finally, "there is my patron. In fact, I had a ride just today. Such a treat. One feels—how shall I put it—practically deified. Borne over all those heads as over a layer of dark clouds..."

What a pair of reactions! A long, gliding, sinuous smile—
and then ice again as she struck the problem. Overflowing with
excitement—how he adored this magnificent model!—he
flung aside his dishes, came striding over, clasped her, and
kissed her hotly on the neck. For with that single truthful word
he'd uttered, *patron*, he'd let her all on her own turn a young
woman into an elderly man. Now she must alter the world to
her will: she must transform that slim olive hand into a withered brown claw, which could not be done.

So with that bit of guiltlessness, of *guile*lessness on his part,
it was accomplished: the next phase of the transformation had
begun. From larva to silk-wrapped pupa, he thought, and soon
we shall have the imago itself. He could not wait to get to work.
It seemed that he must do almost nothing: the marvelous creature conjured it all on her own. Again he clutched her and
kissed her, excited and grateful, just barely managing not to tell
her about this wonderful development, stopping himself with
an uneasy jolt.

8

A cold winter morning some days later, the sky so heavy with
snow that he imagined he could reach up and touch it, Ovid was
following her, as was now usual, while she ran her furtive
errands for Tibo. Since that sighting in the square she seemed to
have made herself believe she'd been wrong, but he could see
how she still resisted, yet how she resisted that same resistance,
and so how her alteration continued. He strode over the slippery stones, keeping her form a short distance before him.
Lucky for his height—otherwise she would be lost among all
the muffled heads. Still, he never knew when she might suddenly stop and glance back over her shoulder. Often, he had to
duck into an alley, to crouch, to press himself against a damp
wall.

Once, as he watched from behind a fountain, he saw her stop
and stare, stricken, at the empty air. It made him start for a
moment, follow her gaze, but he found nothing remarkable.
Now, having slipped carefully behind her again—a quick side-
step behind a column when the crowd slowed and knotted to
look in the shops, and she was so easily distracted by the mar-

velous things in windows—he was watching her wander over the paths of the garden behind the Pantheon. She moved like a firefly following its own secret path. He knew that on these smooth blocks of marble, over which everyone else strode matter-of-factly, were invisible things that impeded her. She paused once or twice, with nothing visible before her, but gathered her dress and stepped around.

The other day she had stood before him and said, "Twins." Just that, patting her stomach. "How do you know?" he asked shortly. She stared at him, incredulous. "They're right there!" she cried, and flung her hands before her, as if only a fool couldn't see. "They've started talking," she added, and merely smiled and hummed when he asked what they said.

Now Xenia stopped at the base of the theater and stared up at its curved marbled side, at all its high tiered arches. As he watched she made a quick, awkward motion, practically shielding herself with her arm. Alarmed, he looked up, half expecting to see that splendid marble monster tumbling down, but it stood there, serene as ever, the thick blanketing sky barely moving behind it. She, meanwhile, had checked the motion, had carefully returned her arm to her side.

Ovid looked at the air, at the emptiness, anew. He searched with all the force of his genius, trying to wring from it any of the subtle substance she saw. If he could just *see* such things as she did—if he could squint and the world would reveal to him whole other layers . . . He stared at the theater, at the paved plaza before him. If only it were just a little more marvelous, that would be enough. If human bodies were not always simply human bodies, the same sizes, the same colors, plodding on the ground. If the world would slip open for a moment—if a fish might swim between the columns, or a woman dart through the clouds, or a shade rush shrieking through this ordinary dull matter, leaving everything transfigured in its wake . . .

But the world did not alter; it did not shudder and crack and transform itself before his craving eyes. It stood immobile, obstinate, dense. The same arches, the same dull staring windows, the same human motions and daily life, all the shuffling across a hard surface. As Ovid helplessly saw only that, an ugly feeling crept inside him, in through his reddened raw nostrils.

When he looked again, he had lost Xenia. He stamped and breathed on his hands. Perhaps she'd spotted him—perhaps she was even pursuing *him* now. He altered his stride, turning himself out. He could well imagine her watching him with those proud, jealous eyes.

It was after lunchtime and freezing, no snow but a fine sleet spitting from the heavy gray sky. He'd have to hurry: he was expected; he was late.

That evening Ovid felt the icy wetness seeping into his clothes, right through the wool and linen and into his shivering flesh, as he hastened home in the sleet.

A feeling of ill will ran through him as deeply as the cold while he skidded, cursing, down the dark street—a discontentment he could not yet define. It was something his patroness had said, up in her splendid chamber, something that had fingered his bones. He'd been reading from act four, only occasionally slipping off and enjoying what he'd written, otherwise much too tense. But as he read she slowly became rapt; he couldn't help but see that. Rapt, with a wondering smile on her face. He began to grow elated, to feel that incandescence. Success, success! That sense of being borne up among clouds, up into the ether . . . But then there was that thing she said, and it had jabbed at his chest and pulled him down.

He battered at the door, was admitted by Persilla, and dropped his wet things into her winglike, withered arms. Wrapped in a blanket, clutching a bowl of hot spicy wine, he went into his study to pace. As the first glow of warmth crept into his feet and nose and aching fingers, he sidled over to the window. Looking out cautiously from behind the curtain, he saw Xenia across the garden, her face white and intent in the lamplight. The chill was burning almost feverishly off, and that discontented feeling sent clenching roots all through his ribs. He dropped the curtain and sat.

Very well, *what* was it she had said, this patroness of his?

He'd been standing there, in that warm, lit chamber with its seabed mosaic underfoot—no, actually he'd been striding; he found it impossible to read aloud standing still. Striding in forceful motions over those whelks and starfish, he became for a time rapt himself. And then it ended; his voice broke off in the middle of the second scene. There was a silence, during which he stood with his face to the window, biting the thick inside of his cheek. It was sickening, that waiting; he swung between caring deeply and not caring at all about what she thought.

But then she made a sound, a little throaty cry, and when he turned, she was all lit up. A torrent of praise, a gush, drenching him with pleasure. Then a quick flurry of hesitant suggestions, so light as to bounce off his hide. But after, as her words rang in the air, she tilted her fine dark head and pondered him.

"She's real," she said. "This character of yours."

He started. Did she know? "You mean she *seems* real," he offered.

She only smiled, slow as a scroll unwinding. "Yes," she gave him at last. "She *seems* so real. As if——" and here her eyes did that trick of squinting and wandering off "——as if you actually saw her. As if you'd touched her. As if you even knew how she'd—taste."

She tossed her shoulders as she said this and let loose a little laugh, looking inordinately excited. She looked as though something were just inside her skin, something whirring itself to life at that very moment, and the sheer heat of it shone through her cheeks. She looked, he saw suddenly, as if she had her own idea in this business, as if his dark current was not the only one flowing . . .

He controlled his face. Now she was mirthful, ecstatic. She threw back her head, flung up her hands, shot one silk-draped leg out before her.

"It's a compliment!" she cried.

A compliment. Ovid's ears rang all the way home, red and burning in the sleeting rain. A compliment to be told that he cannot invent. That he is a copier. That the world around him has become dry and prosaic. That he has grown utterly dependent, no better than the audience itself, on whatever this creature across his garden might reveal—this creature whom he has blackguardly stolen and planted before him, imagining herself an exquisite, rare bloom.

Which, he thought now, grinding his teeth, she *is*. Exquisite and terribly rare. With that clever tongue and those ambiguous eyes that had glided into his flesh as only one other pair of eyes ever had. Oh, god, exquisite, yes. And rare, and rare, and rare . . .

But *stolen?* He had hardly stolen *her.* He rose, went back to the window, and stood breathing heavily at the dense, blood-colored curtains. He hated the smell of wool; his nose twitched. With a finger he poked the curtain aside, just enough for one glaring eye. There was Xenia, lamplit in her room, sitting on the edge of the bed. She seemed to be singing to herself—no, to her belly. To the thing inside her belly. Or *things*—really, twins? Speaking, already? He shut his eyes.

But soon, reluctant, he resumed his gaze. Beside her, by the bed, something was slowly burning, sending up puffs of pinkish smoke. She turned to it, hand still flung in the air, and sniffed, and seemed to approve.

He rested his forehead against the window frame. Yes, he was dependent. He would simply transcribe it as it unfolded before him. He could not help himself.

When he had sailed from Rome last spring, he had never expected anything like this. In fact, he told himself suddenly, opening his eyes with a snap, she had started the whole thing herself. Yes. She'd spun spells, from the very beginning; she had drawn him to her. Probably clear from the Aegean. She'd read all his work. She'd been waiting there, *willing.* For she knew how to do that kind of thing, devilish—god only knew *what* she knew. She even seemed to hint these days, with crafty sideways glances, that she knew what he himself so horribly wanted to know but was much too afraid to ask. If she hadn't done all that she'd done, he might simply have sailed away, leaving her like a perfect shell in the sand.

But she *had* done all that, so he had not sailed away. And what did *he* do to her, anyway? Nothing: he merely watched as she spun herself into herself, and she craved that watching. How was he to resist? He felt himself harden; he felt relieved. So: the fact that she, over there, through the icy wet night, doing and hearing and seeing whatever on earth she did—that

she should be who she was, and how she was, and from where;
and that the other one, up in her chamber, should be exactly
who *she* was, and playing *her* part, regardless of her own idea of
the thing. A princess, and a witch . . . It all kept falling into
place around him, as gently as silent, soft snow.

9

Xenia was sitting in the echoing lavatory of the women's baths some days later, her eyes fixed on a statue's disdainful marble expression, thinking hard about Tibo. From the corner of her eye she could see the two women seated to her right—stately women, their arms quivering with gold as they gossiped away, only the slightest sign of what went on beneath their waists passing over their brows. She shut her eyes but opened them at once. Someone always seemed to be looking.

After wearing the chaplets, breathing the coltsfoot, and choking down the betony, Tibo had finally stopped coughing, but he still had the fever, the headache that made him press his fists to his temples, and that uncanny white ring around his lips. Now whatever had breathed itself inside him was dwelling in his mouth: his tongue was like a strawberry, scarlet and speckled white. And that underground vapor still hung in his room; she could see it hovering at his nostrils, at his hot red ears, thick as fog upon his tongue. It had not begun to disperse at all—she could not believe it—despite everything she had done. The boy writhed with the pain in his head, and she could only stand there, appalled.

Once more she went over her mental list of ailments and the cures that, one by one, had been useless. A shuddering spasm went through her.

Furthermore, Ovid had lied.

At once that terrifying flame flew up, that inexplicable blackness enveloped her, and she shut her eyes, driving her nails into her palms.

But then there came a pair of sharp little kicks. She looked down, startled. For here it was again, out of the blue: that melting that began in her heart and spread through her, like the sun pouring over the horizon, obliterating her thoughts, pulling her up from the clutching black earth, down from the yearning dry sky, settling her here, in this warm globe of life.

"Soon," she whispered. "Soon."

But was someone watching? Only the statue seemed to smirk, but she felt a gaze still on her skin. She hurried into the cloakroom, placed her things in a bundle on the shelf, and walked naked over the wet tiled floor to the baths.

Hovering in the water were the heads and shoulders of women, their breasts bobbing, their hair twisted into elaborate coils. Splashes echoed; there was a morning lull and hum. The fish mosaicked upon the ceiling, the lobsters, starfish, a few darting eels, were reflected on the water's surface so that they seemed to swim. Xenia threw herself into the water, and for a moment she was again gliding through the clear green waves, seeing all the peacock colors that had hovered around Ovid as he hid in the dunes, seeing again how he watched her, enthralled. She shut her eyes and slowly stroked, and when she surfaced she found a woman gazing at her, a woman with heaped-up hennaed hair.

"Can't you stay under a long while!"

Celia? Flavia? Celia. "Practice . . ."

"Ah yes, you lived by the sea."

She was older than she had seemed at the party, and looked simple now, motherly, without her clothes and jewels. She caught herself staring again and laughed.

"I'm sorry," she said, "but you're so very fair." She paused. "You don't have long now, do you?"

"Twins!"

Again Celia laughed, uneasy, and seemed about to say something but didn't. She lifted an arm for her towel to be handed down, and, stepping from the water, smiled at Xenia, a watchful smile. "Then you'll have to be twice as careful," she said.

She padded away, and Xenia floated, seasick, the water falling black leagues beneath her. *Careful.* That roaring began in her ears, that floating off into darkness. *Treacherous.* Someone jumped just then, there was a sudden violent surge in the water, and Xenia's throat constricted. She staggered to her feet.

Other women looked at her; she turned and faced the wall, forcing herself to breathe steadily. She put her hands to her stomach, but after a moment placed them instead lightly upon the water.

Ovid, she thought.

Publius, Ovidius, Naso.

That gaze still passed between them, like ichor in her veins. *I need you.*

What did that woman know about anything?

Xenia climbed from the water, dried herself quickly, pulled on her gown, and bound her boots, suddenly strong again, heroic. Chaste tree, hogweed. She went out into the cold.

Walking north, around the Pantheon and up past Cleopatra's Needle, she reached the spot where Augustus's peace altar stood, a magnificent carved box. A lush marble woman, a swan by her side, plump babies, little flowers curling all around . . . The marble flesh was so delectable, so smoothly polished, that Xenia ran her fingers along the roundness of the arm, over the tender little crease of the stomach. As she touched the stone, images from centuries to come began to glimmer before her: a marble girl, running, frantic, willing to let her own downy arms turn into bark and branches rather than be seized, a painted boy left hanging in sheer air, his wings molten, the feathers falling away . . . Ovid's work, but painted on walls, on ceilings full of sheer apricot light and slate clouds; rooms of statues, their stone flesh live, caught in the moment of transfiguration. Xenia forced the world around her to grow clear again: the marble box, the cold ground, the people shuffling by.

So it was not just that his words would live on for a few hundred years; it was more than that. The bodily, expiring things of the world were transformed by him into words—which themselves would be taken up, millennia later, by other hands, other minds, and transformed once more into voluptuous bodies of color and marble. Sublimation.

Xenia looked at her trembling hand. She had never dreamt this much. This man, this poet . . . He was a god, he would live on. She looked down at her body, transfigured by him, at *herself*, who would be transfigured. Children born of golden eggs! What did Celia mean, *careful*? She knew nothing at all.

Xenia walked around the great box until she was calm, studying the carved images, the rows of somber Romans, the marble animals being led to the altar. She smelled the incense heavy in the air, the sweet smell of myrrh. But from beneath the stones at her feet, mixing with the incense, seemed to rise the smell of blood.

They said the fields of Italy had been soaked with it during the civil wars, before Augustus had become Augustus and taken the city and the world; bits of Roman bone and shards of skull were turned up still by farmers' hoes breaking clods of earth. Afterward, when the wars were over and Augustus had become emperor, the killing had been more discreet; hundreds of senators were ripped out like weeds, silently, night after night. *Slit your wrists, please, in a warm bath,* requested the nightly messenger. *I'll wait until you're done.* She could feel that blood squelching beneath her feet now, bubbling up warm through the paving stones.

Those wars and proscriptions had been when Ovid was a boy; over the memory of all this blood the emperor had laid down slab after slab of marble. And with the marble came the new laws: Augustus had badly lowered the number of Romans, especially the patricians, and so they must be replenished. Hence the selection of promising country boys to come and be made proper Romans; hence the laws punishing bachelorhood, adultery, childlessness, and marriage between Romans and slaves.

All those moral laws, she thought, nearly laughing. Making Ovid burn his work! Yet he would live on for *millennia*! She ran a finger along the processions of marble Romans, so complacent, so peaceful. You certainly would not know, looking at this, about all the blood, she thought. You might not even know about the animals, the thousands denned beneath the city's streets until they were let out, half starved, to devour terrified criminals or be speared in the emperor's shows. Thousands of animals, even ostriches and an occasional giraffe, in addition to

all those panthers. She imagined the creatures shipped up from
Africa, sand-colored lions groaning listlessly in filth, howling at
their losses, starved panthers pacing in dark dens, their eyes
dully red. She could nearly hear them stirring; she could smell
their sick, sweating fur. She looked down at her feet, as if she
might see a crack in the blocks, a pair of wild, desperate eyes
peering up.

She stopped; she whirled: where *was* it? Behind her?

But of course there was nothing, just the stares of passing
faces and that smell that hung in the air. She drew her mantle
over her nose and proceeded, wary, and as she walked along the
emptying Flaminia, she felt the twins inside her, their four eyes
peering ahead.

When she came home, the sun was already setting. She'd
walked far, to where she'd never been, but had found no apollinaris, no peony, no hogweed, just dark eyes at barely opened
doors, eyes upon her in the streets, her own eyes burning with
intent as she moved through alleys as if through passages in the
underworld. Alcestis, she had been thinking fervently as she
hurried along—the Sibyl, and Circe, and Psyche. She felt
heavy, hands and feet swollen and blue, as she reached Ovid's
door. But Psyche, she remembered, was pregnant, too, when she
performed her labors for Amor. And her baby was named
Bliss . . .

Xenia turned the stiff brass doorknob, but as soon as she
entered the atrium she stopped: it was tinged with something,
someone's recent presence. She stood still, arms out at her sides,
fingers touching the air. A light swath stretched from the door
to the screen of Ovid's study, faintly red and warm, like a cloud

of blood in water, dispersing even now. It was a woman: Xenia could smell it and feel it on her skin. A *potent* woman. The house was strummed, as if by a knowing new hand.

Looking beyond the low square pool and tangle of plants to the study screen, she realized Ovid was listening.

10

Ovid had been shocked by that peremptory rap, for no one had been to the house in months. As Persilla had gone to open the door, he'd waited, without breathing, behind his screen. Then he could smell expensiveness; he could hear a silky swishing. There was a pause; he strained. Was it *she*? Was she standing in the atrium, taking in the freakish garden? Flustered, he stood up, knocked over his chair, and saw her at the opening of his screen, her slim olive arms twined in gold snakes, her red-black hair held in coils with long needles. She let her eyes travel about his room.

"You have some remarkable things," she said at last. One long fingertip stroked the painted pearlike flank of a nymph, but her eyes were already peering with interest around Ovid, into the garden, and toward the other wing.

He must have looked discomfited, his stylus still in his hand, long fingers arched protectively above the fresh wax of a tablet. She noted his awkward stance and rustled forward. "I've interrupted you. But I thought I'd simply bring it myself. The walk's not long, as I suppose you know. Just a few ideas I had on what you read me last."

She handed him a red-ribboned tablet and, after looking around for a few more agonizing minutes, left. Then, awful, only moments after the door had shut behind her, Xenia herself returned. She came in muttering, then abruptly fell silent. Ovid found himself sweating, his wrists and palms slick. He felt like a small boy hunched in a closet, with his ears perked and his eyes bright, guilty, excited, straining to follow Xenia's motions. He actually sensed *her* sensing. At his desk, heart beating, he was just able to see her through the slits of his screen, her arms out at her sides, gently touching the air for clues, her face blank in visions. All he could do was wait. And when, after a sickeningly long time, she finally knocked on his door, he burst into a high giggle, swinging his head around in a mannered way, flinging out a welcoming arm.

The room suddenly seemed warm, feverish, and he flushed in the middle of his smile, certain that she could feel it. He dropped his head for her to pet and realized that his scalp was damp. And then, despite the sleepy smile he forced to his lips, despite the doglike pushing of his head against her hand, despite his legs flung out to seem abandoned, he noticed his hand upon the desk, trembling. She touched it with one cold finger, and he watched with horror as it grew still.

After a moment, with a terrible lightness in her voice, she said, "Someone was here."

He looked up, a corner of his mouth helplessly rising. "Yes, as a matter of fact." Composing himself, he scrutinized her, holding her at arm's length between his legs. "Now how did you know that? You've only just walked in; you haven't even seen Persilla. And I doubt my visitor left prints."

She dismissed the question. "But," she said in a moment, with compunction, "I don't know *who* it was."

"Don't you?" He leaned back in his chair and regarded her with a faint smile.

After a moment she extracted herself from between his legs. "I do know it was a woman," she said, and put a hand to her stomach against a kick he could actually see. Fingers oddly curling, she slipped her hands behind her back.

"That you know my visitor was a woman," he said, his own fingers twitching a note to himself, "is remarkable. For she was indeed. As I expect she still is. Simply delivering a letter, however." And with his chin he pointed to his desk, upon which lay the red-ribboned tablet.

Xenia seemed just barely to resist reaching out and snatching the tablet. She remained where she stood, hands behind her back, tongue moving rapidly over her teeth, and he could see the mistake she made, how she trapped herself again in a presumption: that only slaves brought messages, as only men were patrons. And how, making this mistake while knowing what her senses clearly told her, she could not help but think he deceived her.

It made him giddy, the way the whole thing proceeded, the way she spun herself into form before his eyes.

That had been two weeks ago. Still Xenia labored over the cook's boy; he heard her going up and down the creaky stairs, saw her boiling and twining and grinding, wiping oily streaks from her face. She seemed to be collecting breath, filling her rooms with stoppered jars of vapor. Curious, he thought. Yet it made him faintly nervous, what might be in those cloudy spheres. Whatever was inside the boy had begun a sort of corrosion, erupting now in spots and blisters all over his skin. She looked more and more outraged—how she wanted the world to bend to her will! She seemed to believe that this was her

mission, her Hydra to slaughter, her Minotaur—an idea she
had divined or conjured, as she divined or conjured all of this.
But this Hydra had a million heads, this maze had nothing
inside it: children never survived the red fever. It was just a
matter of time.

He could see her alter. The change gleamed sometimes in
her eyes; he swore it even darted at her fingertips and alarmed
her, as if it were foreign, as if it were not all herself.

Some days after that incident in his study, he had come
home with a gift presented by his patroness—just a small
thing, she had said, to spur him on. It was a gold-and-ivory stylus, a treasure—smooth, elegant, and extremely sharp. Ovid
had, of course, recognized its potential at once—gifts are
always dense with significance, their ribbons trailing back to
the fingers of the bestower—but aside from that, his greedy
heart had leapt with sheer delight at its beauty. He was in his
study exploring the clean lines it made in the wax, enjoying
immensely how it cut the surface like water, imagining himself
skimming the sea, when he sensed Xenia just outside, in the
cool sunny garden, watching.

He faltered a moment, stricken, knowing how the world
must shift and shiver before her eyes, while here he sat, toying
with his bauble. He sensed, again, the cold gap between them,
which set her above him in a more transparent, more valent
world, and left him stuck among the dull, the time-caked.
Again he felt himself harden.

He gave no sign that he'd seen her, not even a twitch of his
brows. Aware of his long, elegant, celebrated form and the
effect it always had upon women, Ovid let himself remain in
the pose she had spied, this pose of secret, *significant* pleasure
in his precious new gift. He ran his finger gently up its sleek

ivory side, as he would the bare thigh of his love; he lowered his lids, fingertip slowly circling the gold point, and smiled slightly, as if recalling something most intimate; he drew the smooth ivory shaft over his dry, enraptured lips. And then to his shock he felt a terrible coldness beside him, and, when he looked up, she was gone.

Yet he used that minor incident, he used everything, in the days and weeks that followed. The very temperature of her jealousy, incipient as it was, he measured and converted into words and scenes. From behind his curtain, or through his screen—even squatting one night behind the cold granite herm—he studied her motions, her face. Grinding up concoctions while singing to her belly, she would grimace suddenly, her mind having been seized again. Like a ghost inside her, haunting, consuming, it emerged more and more often.

But all the while he never actually *did* anything. He never *said* anything. He didn't lie. She did it all herself: he behaved with her just as he always had, and it was sincere. Still sighing, still gnawing at her neck, because just compare her to all the others—that lacewing, for instance, so ordinary! Whereas Xenia . . . sometimes her eyes still slipped into his skin and bound him to her in collusion; she seemed to join him in a rarer sphere in which they might both live on. He looked at her and saw two Xenias: one entwined with him in this venture, and the other, who was its subject.

When he looked at himself, though, he saw two as well. Part of him nearly forgot sometimes, nearly clasped her and told her all about his work, how wonderfully it was advancing—but then he remembered and walked away, breathing on his chilled hands.

So her transformation continued.

One night, having been startled awake by the throaty calls of gulls, he thought he heard someone in the atrium. Shivering and clutching his foolish stylus, he crept from his room and down the hall until he saw her, luminous, her eyes wide and unseeing among the dripping greenery.

He held his breath and watched her white fingers grasping for the ferns and slim budding stems. He could hear her breath, the rustlings of the leaves at her hand. And then he noticed the orange cat crouching among the plants. Her hands were drawing slowly near. Her lips parted, her eyes oddly blurred, her hands creeping stealthily closer . . . At last he couldn't bear it and hectically tapped the wall with the stylus. She straightened, looked about her in the darkness, and, with one uncertain hand outstretched, stumbled back to her room.

This subterranean character. Trembling, he imagined a creature curled up inside her as under the soil, pale and membranous, breathing lightly and liquidly, waiting to shake out her damp wings, her fingers wet with blood.

11

Xenia woke with the old chill from her watery nightmare and kicked back the coverlets, frantic, for there had been coils, her legs had been scaly, talons had sprouted from her fingertips, and she thought she had smelled blood. She looked at her body and hands, but everything was clean, even her nails.

Running upstairs, she found that Tibo still burned, despite everything she'd done. He burned, he burned, his small body flushed and diminishing day after day, even the skin on his parched hands peeling. She stared at him in horror, and for the first time she thought she saw death.

The jars: she must keep filling them. But she had subjected dead insects to countless bottles of breath, and nothing at all had happened. Then was it somehow pure light itself? How do you catch pure light? She stood there swaying, at the end of the boy's bed, and thought, There must be something somewhere, a hint I might divine. She would have to try the famous library, see if not everything had been destroyed.

The cool morning air flashed with brilliance, the zigzag path up the Palatine appearing to end in light, the city with all its roofs of baked clay falling away behind her. After the last bend came the blinding plaza, the yellow-veined columns and rows of basalt heroines, the luminous marble box. Augustus's house was up here; she hurried past its portals, feeling exposed—so bright!—and over the wide white steps and into the shadows. Here were the twinned doors, but the Latin library was locked, so she went into the Greek, into its placid coolness. She hovered a moment at the entrance, uncertain.

A man in a shabby cloak came forward. She recognized him—Lucius? Julius?—and was washed with relief. But when she whispered what she wanted, his eyes dimmed, one hand slightly lifting.

"You can look on your own, if you like" was all he said before drifting away, so she settled at a table in a corner and began, dozens of quivers of scrolls around her. Two elderly men turned and stared.

After hours of searching she'd found nothing; she would not find anything here. A small bell rang, and there was a startled scuffling of the other four feet. Stiffly she rose and left the place as Lucius, or Julius, began to swing shut the doors. She came out into the glaring late afternoon and leaned against a column, pressing her hot face to the cool, glossy stone, her eyes stinging with frustration and panic. After a time she pulled herself away, moved dully through the columns and black statues, and climbed the wide stairs to Apollo's temple.

Paintings and objects were displayed on either side of the doors, with statues standing at the center of the porch. There was Caesar's sword, the skin of the snake that had killed Cleopatra, the withered wormy hair of Medusa, Circe's silver stool: Augustus was a collector. As Xenia moved from object to object, examining the paintings and the bronze men's adorned chests, she became aware of the scent of melting wax. She squinted as the shimmering began . . . Then before her hovered rows of tiny glowing white candles, dozens on a rack as high as her waist. She put out her hand, but there was no warmth, only brightness. Beneath her feet lay someone's worn marble bones.

The sun was low, lighting the snaky Tiber to gold, tingeing the plaza's white stones rose. The whole square glowed, incandescent, imbued at that moment by something subtle and living. Xenia stood very still and seemed to hear a singing, as if the twinned libraries were breathing forth their invisible contents, all that had been extracted from life and refined by the brilliance of poets.

So few will remain, she thought, shutting her eyes and listening. But of all of them, Ovid would. Of all this great age, this great Roman world. She could see his face, ancient and boyish, laughing from millennia ahead.

She was at the bottom of history. So much was still to come—billions of lives and thoughts and inventions and wars and all the weighty buildings. Hooves, wheels, feet, and thundering violence would cast over all Rome a fine dust, which would thicken and grow dense and, as the centuries wore on, rise up over this city, over these steps, come creeping over this porch, climb, ever more dense and obscuring, up these fine yellow columns, up to the very pediment, until it had buried those images and words engraved up there in the hope of enduring—until it had hidden them in earth, and of all this world nothing showed but the tip of the highest Egyptian needle, its point interrupting a field of dry grass in which a few cows grazed.

She shut her eyes and opened them again, but the vision had not dissolved. Dust seemed to be falling about her. All over the marble ground, upon her feet, thick and hard to walk through, caking around her calves. The steps' clean edges were covered and lost, the rows of basalt figures and yellow columns themselves half buried, yet the dust still rose. But overhead, laughing, Ovid seemed to flash—a dragonfly, a god.

She stumbled from the porch, down the wide steps, across the plaza, and past the high arch with a statue beside it, a statue of Augustus, or Caesar, or Apollo. She did not see, through all the dust, a figure in silver and blue watching intently as she hurried by.

Xenia could hardly speak that evening in the red dining room, but Ovid was so spirited he did not seem to notice. Over his salmon, a cup of Falernian in his hand, he was intoning lines of Greek. To Xenia, to the fish on his plate, to the watching nymphs and woodland creatures on the walls, he recited line after line of Stesichorus. The words threaded in and out of her ears, that ghostly dust falling about her. When he finished, giving a twirl of his finger and a grateful nod to the fish, Xenia forced herself to be in the room, to speak.

What had he done today, where had he been? She realized he seemed to ponder the simple question, casting his eyes to the nymphs on the ceiling, traveling over their nude flanks one by one. He touched his lip lightly and then swung a pleased gaze back to her. The library, he said. A most thorough day in the library. In fact, he went on, he could hardly string together his own words anymore, so stuffed with those of others was he. Would she like to hear more?

She looked up. "Which?"

"Which what, my sweet?"

"Which library?" But he was quoting Greek, so of course the Greek. Where he hadn't been.

He looked at her, and slowly smiled. "The Latin," he said.

Oh, he couldn't have been; it had been shut. Hadn't it? It was sickening, this fish on her plate. Its silver-pink skin had come loose and clung to the dish; there was a horrid runny drizzle of garum, a dead smell. The sea waves rose in her throat.

He was leaning forward now, while an underworld god reared up on the wall behind him and a girl, screaming, was carried away. He put down his cup and frowned.

"What is it?" How he looked at her! So solicitous! "You're not eating," he observed. "You always eat well. You must eat well. Are you ill? You're not ill?"

But he *was* solicitous—he meant it. He leapt up, plate clattering, and rushed over, crouching before her. One dry palm was on her forehead, another on her arm, those Roman-gray eyes were sincere, searching her own eyes, searching her all over, troubling themselves over her pregnant form as if she were a crystal bowl that must not be permitted to crack . . . Then why lie? The words swam like fish in her throat as he took her arms and petted her. Why turn women's hands into men's? Why, so flush and beaming, proclaim you were somewhere you weren't? And then why be so solicitous?

But did he lie? He *was* solicitous!

"You know," he was saying, "I think you ought to go away. Up to the country house. Away from that boy. I can see it, you know; you're not looking well. The other house isn't plush, but it's comfortable, and it has a fine garden. In fact, you should go for your delivery. It's not far, just up the river, on a hill, much more pleasant than here. And I'll come up every week, gallop up on the horse. You know I'm an equestrian, don't you—" and he smiled as he went on and on, those lean fingers stroking her hair, those warm eyes searching her own stricken eyes, those words so like words he'd used once before. But then, on the pebbled beach months ago, he'd declared that he needed her, and now he was sending her away.

But *did* he lie? He loved her—look! His hands, his eyes, she wasn't wrong! This man who would live on, kneeling before her now . . . How do you resist it, the love of a god, when he's chosen you and needs you?

But then why betray her, why send her away?

She felt, sitting there, legs dangling from the couch, hands clasped in his as he kissed her brow, her nose, her neck—she felt she was tearing apart.

There are two worlds, she thought, but only one is real.

Or was all of this, she suddenly wondered, was all this torment actually a terrible dark zone she was expected to pass through, like Psyche passing through the underworld to heaven? Was all of it part of what he wrote?

PART THREE

1

Julia stood again beneath the cypresses, their fleshy red bark lit with late golden light. She was aware of her mouth, as she always was when outside her grandfather's house—her mouth and all the things she carefully kept inside it, behind the bar of her teeth. For she, like her mother before her, must never say anything not fit to be recorded in Augustus's long scything scroll. She felt them beating at her teeth, though, all the things she wasn't saying, and tasted their bitterness: delicious.

Moving noiselessly among the cypresses and pines of the compound, she looked at the sunlight slanting around her and thought of her summer house. The gardens had risen in tiers, so novel! She'd kept birds in one garden and her great cat in the other, her beloved cat with its sinewy flanks and bluish fur, into which she used to sink her hands. Sometimes she longed to lie with it, to wrap her bare arms around its lean belly, and yes, she would call it a *cat*, *aelurus*, such a lissome word, winding silkily around her hips as she stood in the garden . . . Oh, but every-thing was razed. She remembered Augustus's eyes when he'd ordered it, eyes that he imagined glowed like the sun so that

everyone dropped theirs when they saw him. Did he really have
no idea? The whole house demolished, all that brushwork, all
that marble, all those winding hedges! Her birds had flown up,
bewildered—she could still hear their wings beating the air. At
least she'd smuggled out the cat, and Augustus had no idea she
still kept it.

Just as he had no idea . . . Smiling, Julia crossed the compound garden, plucking needles from a pine, and entered
through the winged doors. She hovered in the musky dimness
of the atrium like a waiting ghost; she had time, handfuls of it.
She dropped a silvery green needle into the impluvium and
watched the ripples form about it. So faint, she thought; so inef-
fectual. She dropped in several more. What does a tidal wave
look like? she wondered. Does the light shine through the volumes of water as the wave rears up above you? Moving slowly
around the square pool, she pricked a needle under her finger-
nail; she slipped one between her teeth. At last she went down
the dark corridor to her room, that one space of color and light.
She closed the door and sat on the couch, settling the pillows
about her.

It was certainly useful, she thought, to have seen yesterday
what she'd seen, precisely how advanced things were. And from
her own gates during her afternoon stroll—how convenient!
Yet she'd been estimating brilliantly—she'd thought it couldn't
be even two months away, and she was right. Yes, everything
was so convenient. For imagine, the perfection: that Aemilius
himself, the monthly husband, had been away the past four
months. He needed a rest, to fight a war, somewhere up in the
north. And didn't he deserve it? He'd performed so splendidly at
home. *Pater, patria*: a new emperor planted.

Which meant that for four months Julia had been almost

free. Only her closest slaves had seen her. She smiled again, pat-
ted her pillows—the silk ones, chartreuse—glanced at her shut
door, and hoped Ovid would not be late.

He was making his way, satchel banging on his back, up the
granite path. Xenia wasn't likely to let herself be bundled away
to the country house, he was thinking, if she was as sickly suspi-
cious as she seemed. Oh no, she'd keep an eye open: she'd sprout
hundreds of eyes, like Argus. Her going away was hardly the
point, but proposing it had been an inspiration. How these occa-
sions fell into his hands! Yet he'd meant it when he said it—
she'd looked so weak, suddenly, so ill. He shifted his bag
uncomfortably, wiping the sweat from his wrists.

The satchel grew steadily heavier, a new set of tablets each
week. He'd finished four acts, had only the most crucial one
before him. It was his own little pregnancy, he thought as he
reached the white plaza at the top of the hill—something born
of his fingers, borne upon his back. The thing was moving,
beginning to squeeze its fat fists, to kick.

Pregnancy, pregnancy . . . He passed through the somber
doors, walked echoingly down the damp corridor, was admitted
to the familiar chamber at the end—and nearly froze at the
doorway. Were they *all* pregnant? Extraordinary that he only
noticed it now, as he greeted her in the formal manner that
belied the hot little current that ran so quickly between them.
But she'd always been seated when she received him, draped
and muffled in heaps of that extremely expensive silk, pillows
all around her. He'd made a point, furthermore, not to notice
her body, his eyes only occasionally straying toward her ear,
silky and alert as a terrier's, with pearls dangling from the lobe;

or lingering for a moment upon the greenish artery that seemed so subtly alive in her neck; or perhaps dwelling briefly on her gleaming dark hair, so artfully arranged with gold needles.

Perhaps it was how she was sitting this time, with her hands folded placidly upon all that crumpled rose silk at her stomach. Did all pregnant women make that complacent, excluding gesture? He could almost smell that warm, milky, satisfied odor pregnant women seemed to give off.

He tried to ignore it as he unpacked his tablets, stacked them with a good, clear clatter upon the round table with silver gryphon legs, cleared his throat, and began to read. He walked forcefully upon the seabed, glancing now and then toward her face. It was excellent that she was pregnant, of course, for now Augustus had another chance at a blood heir. No one could possibly want Livia's slippery sealskin of a son to be the next emperor—even Augustus seemed disgusted by the way Tiberius kept turning up like a worm in dug soil. Yet Augustus had only one blood child, just that unfortunate daughter, from whom he'd reaped three grandsons and two granddaughters before sending her away—on account of her behavior, so they said, but of course everyone looked at plotting Livia. No sooner was his daughter gone than her two eldest boys died, young, and the third was found guilty of something and shipped off. So of all the progeny, that left Augustus with just Julia, here, and her sister. An ugly story, full of darkness—better not dwell on it, especially *now*. Better, indeed, not dwell on Augustus's face as he rides like a dead horseman through Rome—better not think of Livia, gold bracelets twined around her aged, quivering arms, her irisless eyes watching, Tiberius hidden behind her.

No: it was excellent that Julia was pregnant. She need bear just one son, and he need only survive. Ovid could—he could *try* to—summon support in the matter, given that he was invested. Although—here his foot faltered, and in mid-falter he cursed. *No*: he'd been over it a hundred times. Augustus would summon him when he wished; he'd make Ovid wait, put him through trials.

Ovid noticed that Julia seemed to be making a lot of her belly as she listened to him read: she squinted and pondered, working her full, rather snoutlike but appealing mouth, as she often did when she thought, all the while her slim olive hands stroking her stomach like a cat. He felt a twitch of irritation. There was something so sanctimonious, so private in the gesture. Or was she—the thought struck him with the clarity of truth—was she *emphasizing* the fact, so that he noted?

He finished reading the act, exhaled, and stood with his back not quite to her, the echo of his voice melting into the walls.

After a moment Julia cleared her throat lightly. "You know," she said, resting her cheek upon a ringed hand, "she's more and more real. I'm sure I actually see her: her goblin face, how her eyes change like the sky, the way she waits and watches and winds the strands of that tassel around her finger, how she's always whispering, how she creeps unconsciously at night . . ." Julia shivered. "And that intriguing business with her fingertips." Her languorous eyes traveled slowly around the room, dark and dilated. Then, startlingly, she flung them at him. "As a matter of fact, you know, I *do* see her."

Ovid stiffened and nodded, as if it were praise. This torment, again—what did she mean? Was she being literal? Had she actually seen Xenia? Had she seen something that day in his house? He felt all at once that he was being horribly toyed with, nudged by one elegant paw.

Julia was slitting her eyes in a long gaze, a smile hidden in her swollen mouth. With her eyes so narrow and sharp that he felt them slide inside him, she went on. "So," she said, and paused. "I'm dying of curiosity. Are you really going to play it all out, to the end?"

He stood stunned, as if he'd been struck. Did that answer it? Did she know? How could he possibly answer her, here, out loud? He'd never quite asked it of himself, never put it in such short, violent words. The *end*, that unimaginable end to what he wrote . . . But that, of course, was the problem: it was unimaginable; he simply could not envision it, and that was why he did what he did, why he was forced to watch.

He moved about nervously, his long fingers clutching the sticky tablets, aligning them, stacking them, fussing with the ribbons. He was conscious of saying something vague, of falling back once again upon artistic prerogative, the silent sanctity of invention.

"I'll just wait, then," Julia said with what might have been irritation, her slim foot in its gold-threaded slipper jogging quickly. But at once she was smiling again. "There would, of course, be a certain amount of time one *must* wait, wouldn't there?" she said then, resting her hand once more upon her globing stomach.

There was a noise in the hall, and she started and rose. But Ovid took the occasion to flee—his tablets barely tied together and clattering like teeth in his satchel, his footsteps echoing as he hurried into the chilly atrium, through the entrance, under the arch, and out.

A certain amount of time one must *wait* . . . So she really knew, then, that the other, his model, existed. And knew how the whole thing would proceed, how it had to, if the model was to be a real model. As his feet slapped down the dark granite path, his thoughts clicked like the beads on an abacus. He wouldn't go home; he would walk, think it through. He must finally face it.

Impregnation: he tried to be rational. The usual belief held that the female body was merely the shelter, the male influx being the gust of life, the flying *genius*. No, he thought firmly, as he loped beneath a thunderous sky that looked ready to fall or break. He didn't believe it; he had never believed the ancient idea that the female was only the jar. It was inconceivable (he wanly noted the pun). No. The female alone was the one who concocted it. All the male did was a little ploughing, a little sprinkling of rain. So any child born would be *hers*: made of her seed, her soil. Any child—or whatever it was. And so whatever she did to it would have nothing to do with him.

Oh, but this went against what he believed about *anima* and *genius*, his other voice cried as he hurried through the wind across the plaza. He didn't believe—he couldn't believe—that the child was not his as well. Of course it was his. And what would become of it if—as Julia had just so brutally said—he played the whole thing out, to the end?

Then why not just stop? The thought came to him as he crossed the square and approached Augustus's great temple, and it stopped him cold. The wind kept hurrying, though, tugging at his cloak so that it blew before him in the wild flashing darkness, the air stinging his greyhound ears. Why not just stop, get out of this now? Start something new, do something else with this remarkable creature . . . Be clean again, and innocent.

Oh, and lose this patron! Which was all he'd wanted, all he'd needed. The very sight of Augustus's cold white monument made him quaver. Recollect where you were a year ago, it seemed to say: that stony eye watching, your earlier book burned and scattered. Whereas now: you're *in*. With the emperor's own family! Lose this miraculous patroness and you'll be back where you were—no, worse. If she dismisses you, you will be finished.

Ovid stood alone in the plaza. The marble beneath his feet and all the marble before him and towering around him was deathly pale and cold. He could be in a tomb.

Panic bit at him, savage, and he forced himself to move. Away from this barren cold place, these barren cold thoughts. Through the high arch, up into the Subura swarming with life, its gutters rank—but enough to bring his focus back to this plane, this sublunary plane, of flesh. Sweet, firm flesh! For Xenia could be sweet, he suddenly remembered. How her eyes could melt him, how her touch sent fire through his limbs . . . He had cast everything against her, casting her into this role. He admitted it bitterly: this was *not* all her doing. How could it be?

Suddenly he could taste her skin at the tip of his tongue, feel at his cheek the warm hollow of her hipbone and the fine down on the small of her back. And now that she had this tiny thing, or things, nestled inside her, creatures she actually sang to, still hidden . . . Ovid felt stung with tenderness, utterly undone, ready to renounce his great ambitions and plunge his head finally under.

He turned, hurried back over his route, took the path that ran between the twinned hills, and soon he had reached his house, so solid against that wild, flashing sky. Rain splashed in the impluvium as he swept through the atrium and across the blowing wet garden, impelled by warmth and desire.

————

Moments later, his satchel had been dumped on Xenia's floor, his wet boots kicked off, and her knees and palms were bearing into the couch, his bewildering hands clasping her as if for his very life. Violent waves began to break inside her, and in the heat and confusion those tormenting visions again rose—a marble thigh pressed by a marble hand, an apricot ceiling emblazoned with Io and her sad brown eyes, and poor monstrous Pasiphaë, and weeping Myrrha—and what was he doing with *her*, why this torment?

At last the waves died down, and the room returned, enclosing them once more in stone floor and cool walls. Xenia lay with her hand upon his stomach as it rose and fell. His hand covered hers. She shut her eyes and longed simply to see *in* him, see through her palm, read his secrets like a pulse. His breaths came and went more slowly, and the warmth of his skin seeped into her hand so that she felt it nearly glowing while the rest of her grew cool. Yet she saw nothing. Outside, silent lightning flashed, the wind blew, twigs scraped wet twigs.

But she'd noticed when he came in—through the waves and the visions and the hair tangled at her eyes—that when he dropped his satchel a tablet had slipped out.

She waited. His breaths were slower, deeper, his hand upon hers now lax and lifeless. He seemed at last to be asleep, head thrown back, cheeks hollow. She rose, silently pulled on her dress, and tiptoed to the window, where the satchel lay.

At once there was a sense of something from the bed, not a motion but a consciousness added to the room, as if his eyes had opened and lightened the air. She paused, crouching, one hand rooting her to the cool floor in the dark. He was silent; his breaths came and went. She waited as the quiet grew, swelling all around and mingling with the dark, until she felt her own

eyes staring wide and white, and her thighs began to ache. Still
he did not move or speak. At last she heard him breathe as he
did in his deepest sleep, resentfully, submitting even to this
brief extinction only with reluctance. She rocked on her heels,
her belly heavy upon her strained thighs; outside, the palm
fronds whistled. Flickering light fell upon the tablet, scoring
the etched letters. She leaned closer. Carefully, she put out her
hand. She reached for the tablet and began to slide it silently
toward her.

"Don't you know"—his voice split the darkness—"the
story about the girl who shouldn't have opened the box?"

Xenia stood abruptly, tying her sash.

He propped himself up on one elbow, and she could feel him
looking at her with the slow, kindling interest that said that
upon her skin, inside her mouth, and within her eyes was what
he most wanted, what he could not do without, what he would
make live on.

2

Ovid was alarmed. Just when he'd been so tender, when he'd been ready to abandon the whole enterprise! After that night he kept his scrolls and tablets with him always. Even locked doors could not be trusted, for who knew what barriers she could slip through, how she might extract a key from Persilla or drug Lida or Lazar. *Control every subtle thing, penetrate every solid.*

Oh, but the subtle things were slippery, weren't they? This red fever was so quick and metamorphic: it raced through Tibo's small body, occupying a portion and then leaving it ravaged. First the ghostly ring around his mouth had slipped inside, forming the strawberry blisters on his tongue, and then it had gathered and swept through him in raging heat, finally erupting as pustules all over his thin arms and legs, even stripping the skin from his palms. This morning Drusa ran shrieking down the stairs, for the wall far opposite the child was spattered with vomit, Tibo himself lying limp—as if it were the expulsion not of the boy but of the demon that had seized him.

Xenia moved coldly through the house with her jars full of

breath and light, and created shocking combustions in her room. She was somewhere else altogether, Ovid thought, somewhere dark, deep in her imagined mission, killing Minotaurs, slaying dragons, glancing at him over her shoulder. *Are you watching?*

Indeed he was. He studied her constantly from his desk, long fingers latched beneath his chin. The sun shone stronger now, much warmer; today was truly the beginning of spring. A ray of light lay across the table, and he regarded the colors it lit to life. The shot-silk cushion upon which his elbow rested, a somber thing in the shadows, was utterly transformed by this light, the magenta and lime green made iridescent. He pondered the golden glow the sunlight lent the skin of his arm, how the fine hairs gleamed, how even the black wax of his tablet seemed, in the sun, to glisten with light. He gazed at the transformative ray, at the motes dancing within it, shut his eyes, and tried to hear them sing.

But of course he did not; he did not hear such things. He opened his dull, time-caked eyes and looked toward Xenia's rooms, toward her glass alembic and *kerotakis*, her vaporous jars, her glinting vials of beloved mercury, the precious pigments she'd divined somehow inside the dullest minerals. He heard again her voice by the sea, whispering her spells and her secrets, unwinding like a golden thread. And for the first time he wondered—with a pure wonder, with no desire to steal—what she really looked for, and how she would know if she found it.

The stylus in his hand was suddenly hot, the gold tip burning his finger. He considered it from far away, feeling himself divide. Part of him watched as the surface of his tablet began melting in the sun, the slanting words running together, slipping from the life he'd given them back into silent wax. Like the river Lethe, he thought, as one word after another slid into liquid darkness. Like the crumbling sandbanks of that rivulet by the sea. He rubbed his lips together, watched a whole line melt away, and, for a long, suspended moment, in which he nearly felt his sinews loosen, his self go slipping free, he imagined his work dissolving. Into liquid darkness, like this; or perhaps it was into light. But slowly that other self grew conscious, gripping his flesh and sinews tightly. Ovid leaned forward, loosened a tassel, and let the curtain fall.

Sitting in the darkness, he listened to the occasional echoing drips in the atrium. After a moment, he heard Xenia's footsteps. She went out, the opening door sending through his slitted screen a brief shower of light, which disappeared with a click.

Suddenly he felt sickened. He stood up, shoved the tablets and bundles of scrolls into his satchel, and went with it out into the sun.

The men's baths: sanctuary. Luckily, Carus was not there, his cocky head nowhere among the skulls that bobbed, intoning, in the water. With his clothes and the heavy satchel deposited on a shelf, Ovid felt relieved and bare, almost like himself again, lean and brown and unencumbered. As he lowered himself into the hot water, among all the rumbling voices and slapping feet of men, he longed to be one of them again. For he was not; he was monstrous, set apart. He swam listlessly on his back, trailing drops with his fingers. Floating, he waited to sink.

As Ovid, having climbed, shuddering, from the cold baths, slipped into his clothes and hurried up the Palatine, Xenia walked slowly back to the house. She had been wandering by the river, aimless. Tibo continued to shrivel and burn, but she had found no pharmakal or magical means that would save him, nor the precious *essentia* that might. She would never find it, although it seemed—so tormenting—to be almost in view, to murmur at her ear. She had discovered dozens of colors inside the most unpromising materials, but what could color, even light, really do, though it seemed to make stone sing? And the exhalations of all the metals, of mercury and copper and lead: they transformed each other but did nothing to the dead insects. She did not know where else to look, what else to do.

And this torture with Ovid—watching her, goading, yet betraying her still . . . There were, she'd begun to think, only two possibilities. Either these torments were strewn before her like temptations—like subjecting antimony to such violent heat that it was forced from black to green to white, before turning to gold—and so all of it was part of his work, part of how she was being modeled; or else the torments were genuine—in which case the ground beneath her dissolved.

Inside, Xenia found the house silent. She stood in the atrium for a moment and listened: he was not home. She passed noiselessly around the impluvium, among all her twining, breathing plants, her blood beating in her ears. He couldn't possibly keep carrying it around; there were dozens of scrolls and tablets by now. Silently, she went down the hallway, her belly heavy, parting the darkness with a tentative hand.

His room was cool and dim. So like him, she thought, with its spareness and mocking skeleton—a place for him to conceal his ignominious sleeping. Yet even now it was full of his consciousness, full of the scent of his olive skin and the salt-shot hair she could nearly feel at her imagining fingertips. One of his mantles had been flung over a chair. It looked odd, dragging on the floor—when it was usually so animate, a billowing

extension of his form. She thought of the hollowness that must
be in him. Imagine, she thought, if he knew what I knew.
Sometimes she forgot that he didn't, that he lived and worked
within a dark shell of time, not knowing that he would crack
through it.

On the small horse-legged table by the bed lay a pair of
tablets, one upon the other, tapped there until corners met corners by a long finger before the lamp was blown out. She lifted
one gingerly, as if it were a living thing.

All these dark scratches, peaks and ripples, waves impressed
in black. Wind, war, shouting, ocean, the clamor of steel: she
read on, hurried, conscious of time. But on one etched black surface, on another, appeared not a single woman; it was all war
and proclamations, men and speeches and pomp. She felt nothing, reading it, no revelation, no strumming sense of hearing
his words whispered into her mind, as she'd heard them back by
the sea. *Oh god, please don't let my name, my work, sink into
oblivious waters . . .*

In fact, she realized with alarm, what she was reading was
dull. But the instant she formed the thought, she became aware
of a scent in the room, and a watching presence.

He leaned in the doorway, his head at an interested angle.

"There's not one story," he said, "but at least two, about
girls who open boxes they shouldn't." He stepped forward and
dropped his satchel. "Besides, that's not me. It's Carus."

"Carus?" With his step had come a waft of that smell, and
she was horribly conscious of sniffing like an animal and of his
looking with interest as she did so. But she couldn't help it: the
smell was on him, in his cloak; it came floating toward her,
sickening, that sweet, excited animal smell. She had to breathe;
she stepped away.

Like a crow he watched, all beak and blinking black eye, as

she put her hand to the wall for balance. Then he flung his cloak upon the bed, sat, pulled off one boot, and looked up at her with a generous smile. "So did you like it?"

"Like *what?*" Her innards were swimming; she turned toward the door for air.

He gestured at the tablet. "Carus. You know who he is, I think."

She laughed a little wildly, seeing again that figure with arrogant shoulders and dust falling upon him. Shutting her eyes, nails in her palms, she fought the streaming waves and the saltiness in her throat. But inside something struggled to be free: a spitefulness, hot and green.

"Not only do I know who he is," she said, "but I know he'll be forgotten."

The words shocked her. But at once a calm seemed to descend, a fresher, bracing air.

Ovid, though, had gone pale, one long hand falling dead upon the coverlet. An inflated flush ran over his face, then a tight constriction; she kept her own face waxen and hard. At last he laughed, dry and barking.

"You don't know that."

"Of course I do." Now she laughed, incredulous. "I saw it. No one will remember him. Not a word he writes will survive." And, saying that, she ran a toe over the skeleton and left.

As she reached her door and met the sly, laughing eyes of her bronze mermaid, she could scarcely believe what she'd given away, or how extraordinarily exultant she felt.

3

It went into Ovid like a spear, when she said that. Or as he imagined a spear would feel: swift and shuddering, the black shaft obliterating all sensibility, rooting him to the ground.

He couldn't face Carus at all now, couldn't bear to. He skulked, avoided the occasional meetings at the baths, found himself going to others that were inconvenient and far away—but thought about him incessantly. The image mixed with his bedclothes and with the damp air that pried like fingers into his room night after sleepless night: Carus gone under, soft ash rising up his legs and bending sides, under his arms, over his shoulders, nestling around his straining neck as a mother might tuck the sheets around a child . . . Ovid woke up gasping, his hand clawing at his throat.

The fact that she *knew*. And went around daily knowing, keeping those flickering visions tucked neatly inside her eyelids and her spiteful mouth. To know that she *knew*, that when she looked at him—god, he had thought with *love*—a whole other vision danced behind him like a skeleton, laughing with long yellow teeth.

Yet perhaps . . . she knew something marvelous? Perhaps she did love him, because she saw——

He shook his head hard in the mirror. He didn't dare think it. Because if that was so, then why not just tell him? If she loved him? How much could it possibly cost her to tell?

More likely she did not love him at all, but laughed at him, knowing what she knew, and watched him day after day bent over his work, blundering in the dark, spending his life on nothing.

Why do you care, why do you care? The face in his mirror was desperate, demanding. Why can you not just *live*? His white eyes scraped the edges of the room in the wan morning light, scraped and scraped for the answer.

Because living is nothing. Unless you live on, you may as well never have lived at all.

Oh, but there are ordinary means of achieving the same thing, Ovid told himself as he went plunging into the city. Look around——here in the Subura, for instance, in the shops and stalls and crowded streets——look at all this fructification, these quilted damp greens and shining round onions and sweet little bloodred cherries. Look at these babies, the newest versions of long lines of ancestors, whose masks are arrayed on the family altars at home. *That* is what one does; that is what ordinary people do. Look at how that woman there, between the dangling rabbits, gazes enraptured at the small girl plumped upon the counter, seeing in the child's squashed, toothless face her own husband, herself, her favorite aunt, a whole sea of people condensed in this latest little drop. And on and on is how it would go: one drop after another would be pushed forward, as at the end of an icicle, a representative of those behind it, containing all the same substance.

Why is that not enough? Why is that not enduring enough?

Because, he nearly laughed, passing a long, thin hand over his dry mouth as he glanced above the heads of the mob. Because it may be much the same substance, but still it would not be *me*.

Perhaps he'd already done it, already assured himself a place somewhere above all that drifting fine ash. With his *Loves*, his *Art of Love*, and now his *Metamorphoses*—could he already be safe?

Ask her, he said to himself as he stood before the mirror on a morning that was truly spring. He looked at the bristles on his cheeks, barbs of white age poking through his brown skin. When he drew back his lips, his long teeth gave the first glimpse of skull. He shut his mouth, rubbed his lips quickly.

He couldn't possibly ask her. He couldn't bear to know.

And why should she tell him? And what if she lied? Could he trust those bicolored eyes, that clever little mouth? Because once he asked her, and she saw his great weakness, she'd have him; she could twist him like thread around her fingers. And would.

No, he could not bring himself to do it. He'd have to keep soldiering on, in the dark, in his glorious human ignorance. He'd have to push this play on, push it out.

All the way to the end, as Julia had said? That unimaginable end . . .

Xenia had told him. *This* one, this monster, would be his best. And she had cast herself into it!

Then yes: all the way to the end.

It is a larva, he thought insistently as he sat at his desk and

scratched the first words of the second-to-last act into the
black wax. Outside, the garden softened, sprigs of fresh oleander bursting from leathery stems. The thing inside that
swollen creature over there, he thought, is nothing but a pupa.
It is a white, inching, fat, blind, mouthing thing, not human,
not to be taken into account. They're dispensed with all the
time! Women are constantly poking bitter dissolving pellets
of herbs into themselves; stabbing their inner parts with needles; or soaking themselves in scalding water, leaping until
the little parasite comes dribbling out. It happens all the time
while the things are still stuffed inside—so what's the difference in a month, a few weeks? Just the scant difference
between one side of thin skin and the other. What would be
the difference in just waiting until it was out in the air, and
then delivering the blow? Just time—and what's time? Bits of
nothing.

It was not as if she herself would be hurt. It was not as if *he*
would do anything.

He wiped the moisture from his wrists. It was growing hot
now in the sun, the light yellow and strong, spring breezes
blowing in the window, bearing the countryside's rich smells.
He put down his stylus and shut his eyes. He had been born
there, among the lush hills where the breezes arose, in Sulmo.
He could nearly smell it: the fields just turned, all that dark,
rich winter rot let out into the warm air, the melted streams
rushing through muddy banks. And in those spring breezes,
when he was a boy, had lurked as well the smell of the blood
that had soaked the fields during the wars. So many men cut
down, worked in pieces back into the earth, or burned into the
sky. All for the ruthless ambition of that cold marble man up
there on the Palatine.

Ovid opened his eyes and looked at his long hands lying, palms up, in a pool of sun. Was he himself really so ruthless as to go through with this thing?

If he knew what he so desperately wanted to know, would it make any difference? Would it allow him to stop?

4

Xenia saw how he looked at her with craving eyes, his unasked question hanging before him, and she was filled with a warm, seeping strength, knowing that just inside her mouth was the knowledge that would transform him. She felt she'd emerged from the underworld, a place where she'd spun dangerous visions from air. All those temptations: she had survived them. The black and green had burned away, and now she felt herself glowing silvery white . . . As if she had been heated to incandescence and tempered. She was more than herself now, polished, heroic, her vision clearer than ever before.

Tibo's disease changed form again, moving to his brain. For days he chattered nonsense words, his voice as shrill as a bird's sometimes, then shockingly low, like a frog's. Xenia saw Drusa's hair rise. But she looked in the boy, saw the ghost clearly, and knew what to do.

She gathered sulfur, bitumen, mastigia, and lotus pith; she wrote the commands upon scraps of tin; and, pulling the bed-sheets from the boy, she whispered the words and blew . . . Down his thin, bare body, which writhed at the touch of her breath; then up, provoking and enraging the monster inside so that it finally burst from the boy's mouth, runny and wild. At the sound of his gagging shrieks and the smell of the noxious smoke rising from Xenia's pot, Drusa ran from the room, her cloak over her eyes.

Smoke hung in the air, an underworldish smell; Xenia wiped the boy's fouled mouth. But it had worked. His body softened. A childish look returned to his face, and he drifted peacefully to sleep. How he slept: it must do him good. Xenia opened the window to the spring air. It was a marvelous sleep, angelic.

Again the light was strong and warm, the tints of her jarred powders and petals falling in colored pools upon the floor, pools that almost sang. The garden put out shoots, pointed tips breaking the ground like tiny soldiers, secret juices in the new stems and the tightly packed buds. There was promise underground, a green potency that might be pulled up in her hand. And that elusive *essentia*—she felt it all around her; it seemed to ring in her ears; light itself took on dimension. She felt it slipping inside her, like Semele's lightning, like Danaë's gold. It would come to her, she was certain—she was on a trembling edge.

Ovid was again as he had been. He hovered near her, eyes drinking her in.

Surely his work was nearly done? He tapped his stylus often, chin in hand, gazing into the light. He studied a tablet, made a mark, then unmade it, and looked away.

The thought came to her that his work and hers would be done together, just as they both often cried out at once, everything melting between them, nails in each other's skin. At the moment she found what she sought, the moment she wrenched this rarest secret from the elements, his greatest work, too, would be done. That was when she would tell him, when they were both safe.

———

But how would she tell him? She giggled, just thinking it. Would she lead him through the city and say, *Here, and here— you won't believe it—will be palaces with walls and ceilings all covered with images of your stories, with your words, even, painted in gold! And there, on that hill up the river, will be the most gorgeous halls filled with sculptures of your characters, so vivid, so like flesh! And not just in Rome but in palaces beyond the smoky hills to the north, and farther, in cities and countries that haven't yet risen... In small dark cells far beyond the Alps, a thousand years from now—imagine—men will be bent over you, taking pains to put down your words with a flourish, taking such pains that the thin line that is your work, your life, will stretch on forever...*

How she would tell him—she could hardly wait. But only when it was over, and they were both *fixed*. She would present it to him as a prize. And the babies, the babies! They would come then, too! And be plumped here in the garden, a little Ovid, a little Xenia, sunlight on their marble skin, a whole new world of delight... She put her hand to her stomach, shut her eyes in that melting wave, and imagined how she would dispense her gift: throned, golden, the babies in her arms—the personification of richness and magic.

Yes, you will live forever! We will!

Tibo slept on, his silky lashes making fringes of blue shadow beneath his sleeping eyes. The lashes fluttered occasionally; the little moist mouth sometimes opened. But still he slept and slept, so deeply: it must be doing him good.

Inside Xenia, the twins stirred and kicked. Oh, it was near.

They would be coming in a month, they must be. But they were anxious about it sometimes, she felt; they seemed to cower inside her, to shrink from the day. So she soothed them and sang softly until they dreamed. She could see them already, with their downy heads and dimpled bottoms and slender, fragile necks. She could imagine exactly how they'd feel in her arms, the weight of their heavy heads in her palms. Her back arched as she envisioned them, her teeth lengthening, mouth snarling, her body protecting those two little creatures clamoring for milk.

5

Finally, one warm night, when the bedclothes seemed rough-
ened and salty, Ovid could no longer endure it. He flung the
covers off, threw his greyhound legs out of bed, and walked
down the musty hall to the study. He stood there a moment in
the moonlight, naked to the nymphs all around. Outside, the
garden stirred, dark and moist, its secret green blood flowing.
Spring can always be smelled most at night, he thought, when
the earth opens its damp wings. There is always hope, then, and
imaginings that come flying in and try to carry you off.

He stepped into the garden and gazed up at the sky, filling
his lungs with night air. Suddenly he was his younger self
again, a boy just arrived in Rome from the sleepy hills of
Sulmo. He remembered those first months, the very taste of
them on his tongue: how he'd bent over his lamp at night, and
how he'd pushed away his books and blown out the lamp and
wandered into the streets of Rome. He barely slept in those
days, gliding with eyes wide through the winding streets and
gleaming colonnades; he pressed his cheek to a glossy column;
he shut his eyes at the sheer, painful pleasure of the beauty in

women, in objects made of stone and gold, in color brushed upon plaster. And one evening, in the grand hall of the baths, he happened to hear Horace.

Shutting his eyes now, he could feel it again, as if the soft spring night air took on that fabulous delicacy. He could hear Horace speak, as if measuring out something fine; his words, Latin illumined with Greek, were somehow made of porcelain, glass, earth, dry wine, soft skin, a girl's quick laughter. They hung in the air when the poet paused and seemed to *become* the things they meant, intact and round. Ovid had stood among the listening crowd, and as Horace reached the end it seemed that the veils were almost drawn back, the air nearly revealed a fineness he'd never sensed before, so fleeting he could not grasp or name it, save that it was the breath of human meaning itself.

Years passed. That air always hovered just above him; he was a dog snapping at far-hanging fruit. Horace died, and Vergil died, and even sweet Tibullus died. Ovid wrote his elegy, sobbing, for he so wanted to be like Horace or Vergil, he so wanted to do it right. And in all those years he roamed the streets, staring into people's faces, into their rooms and the blinds of their smiles, but he was always apart, caged in his own laughing self, unable to crack through his own glazed surface and enter the air in which Horace and Vergil had dwelled.

And, too, there was Corinna.

He'd seen her the other day, by chance. Older now, but a spear had gone through him all the same when she turned in the middle of a portico. Her age was the exquisite, refined variety only rare women achieve, experience having clarified the lovely features he had so adored. A smile left over from whatever she'd been saying lingered on her face when she turned and saw him, her lips slightly open. And it seemed to him, in that silent moment, that she said something with her eyes, that she even *forgave* ... Then she turned away again, as she had always turned away, and reentered her life, disappeared.

But that moment when she looked at him, he thought his heart would tear. For the light falling upon her through the columns was so like the light, the shuttered light, that had fallen softly upon her bare body that afternoon long ago.

His Corinna. A hundred poems, desperate poems, hammered with roses to her door. Poems that had slipped at last into the sheer dream that she loved him, would always love him, and her glance had not turned to dust in his hands.

Ovid realized that he was standing in his dark garden, naked. He looked down at his body, moved one foot upon the portico's patterned floor, and wobbled a pebble with his toe. A breeze stirred, and he stood still, hearing the spring air among the new leaves, hearing the palm trees rustle.

There must be hope, he thought. He must try. He must at least try to know, and to save himself, and her.

He gathered himself and moved through the portico, inside the damp walls, to her door. He touched the mermaid handle—how long since he'd first held its tiny waist and swelling scaly hips! Standing in her room, he felt it was almost as it had been, months ago, when he had crept toward her house by the sea. This mosaicked floor could be pebbles, and that moon could be the same moon that had laughed down at him, shedding chalky light upon her arm and the grimy sole of one foot. He himself was the same, still the thief, casting a shadow upon this sleeping young woman, her middle so shockingly swollen. For *she* was no longer the same.

If she would only tell him what she knew.

But oh, if it were the worst. If she were to open those strange eyes and shake her head, tell him now he was already nothing, that there had never been any point . . . She would extinguish him utterly.

But then—wouldn't he be free? Wouldn't he be able to let go his wretched grip on the sky, let himself fall, and *live*?

What if she said not that but what he so feverishly wanted to hear? The thought squeezed stinging tears from his eyes. If that windy transformative thing had already won him what he so wanted—couldn't he let himself live? Couldn't he surrender this monstrous task?

"Ah, god, just tell me!" he said, and fell sobbing upon her.

To Xenia, still asleep, he was the breeze, the white dove in a beam of light, flown miraculously in her window.

But he was crying! She struggled to wake. He was burying his face in her throat, his hands clutching at her under the bed-clothes. Her neck was wet with his tears, as, wordless for a time, the sheets were pushed away and their limbs began to twine and she felt her soft nighttime body start to tighten, to wind. But, in the middle of it, what was he saying? Into her neck, again and again—"Please just tell me," he wept. "Tell me what you know."

What she knew . . . Her treasure, her secret. The visions sprang up before her again, as her body rose against his, all clamoring and agitating to get out—those painted boys, those monks' white hands, those apricot ceilings, those silver clouds. They jostled and strained at her heart, pushed at her teeth, and she felt herself almost break open.

But then what would she have? For in all those visions, she did not yet see herself. She closed up like a box with a key.

Because, she realized, confused tears streaming down her own cheeks as everything began to melt inside, she could be saying it, too—she could be weeping the same words as he. *Just tell me—what are you doing with me?*

The moment came, and shuddered between them, and gradually died away. They lay still, their two hearts cooling in the dark. Ovid turned his head after a time, and his eyes settled upon hers. Then he touched her face, his wet fingers fumbling at her cheeks and damp mouth, coaxing it, nudging it open as if it were the petals of a rose.

"Please, just tell me," he whispered.

She took in her breath, parted her lips—but then shook her head.

He lay there awhile, dead, staring. Then he got up from the bed and walked quietly away, gray and naked in the window.

6

The next morning there was a silence like a hole that Xenia sensed the moment she woke. The life within the house was lessened, one small measure withdrawn.

Upstairs, Drusa sat stonelike at the end of the narrow bed, tears slipping down her yellow cheeks.

Xenia stood once more above the little blanketed form. The same sticky black lashes, the same curl to the mouth, the same roughly cropped skull. A small boy, not yet six. She held a hand above his nose and mouth, trying to imagine that breaths or childish words still came floating up. But the bottom of his deep sleep had been so shifty, so soft, it had been effortless for him to fall through.

After a time, she left the silent mother, the empty room, and went downstairs, fingers trailing along the walls. Watery plants grew from the pots in the atrium; in the garden, green blades came stabbing through.

The light in her room was blue and cool. She sat at the table, laid her hands upon the smooth wood, and stared vacantly out the window. On the shadowed side of a column, a chameleon slowly darkened. The orange cat lay sunning by the herm; it sighed and stretched, one white paw reaching out, claws curving into the warm air.

After a time Xenia heard a humming in her ears. She felt she was slowly understanding. Her hands upon the table began to tremble; around her, lights seemed to glimmer.

Of course Tibo had not survived. She'd heard Persilla once, and ignored her: children never survived this red fever. She'd been so determined that she hadn't understood, but now she saw: the real task still lay before her, its nature clear.

She must do it tonight, as soon as it was dark. She'd need dolls made of dough, which was easy, as she knew the small form by heart: the squareness of his fuzzy head, his thin ribs, his monkey hips. Two small dough dolls, identical. And two snips of his hair, some tiny thin nails, quite a lot of laurel, honey, milk, and wine. There would have to be two deep pits; her eye focused upon the bright garden. No: outside the city walls, where there was more darkness and space. The blade of her knife, she noted, must be sharpened. That long cut itself Drusa should not see; perhaps her eyes should be bound. And the smoking as the fresh juices met the ones already secreted by death—the mother should not see that either. She'd need the cat, too, of course: it rolled as her eyes fell upon it, giving the sun its white belly. And all her vaporous globes.

The whole day lay before her; at least she had that. Luckily she'd brought white false hellebore and wormwood, for she'd never find them in Rome. But some of the simpler things—the fresh laurel, the fennel seeds—she must get, right away.

Her mantle swung from her shoulders; her worn basket swung at her arm. As she hurried into the blinding garden, the cat looked up with startled green eyes and sprang into the lavender. She'd have Lazar catch it. Her heart pushed into her throat, and she felt a trembling in her elbows and knees, a terrible desire to fly. Persilla was coming out now; Xenia would have her make sure they washed Tibo carefully but did not yet cut that wisp of hair, and, above all, did not clean his mouth.

Ovid was with Persilla, talking to her quietly. The old woman's cloudy head was bowed, her fingertips touching her dress. Xenia hurried toward her, her voice flying ahead with her orders, but Ovid stepped forward, stopping before her on the path.

They looked at each other, in the strong light, and for a moment Xenia felt that they were back on the blowing pebbled beach and he was whispering into her hair. She looked at him, in the sun, and smiled as she'd smiled then, showing that she understood. His face was dark in the bright light, his shadow falling upon her.

"I have to hurry," she said.

He seemed to study her, his head tilted.

"There's not much time," she whispered.

"Time . . ."

"To bring—" She paused. But of course he knew.

"To bring him back," he said softly.

She could not see his expression, his face at an angle and shadowed, but he was silent a moment, the fingers of one hand stroking the air.

"Yes," he whispered after a time. "Resurrection."

Resurrection. She heard its splendor and violence, the word itself ripping open the earth. She realized she was trembling, and nodded, but again felt herself flung back to her shore, standing with him in his sky-blue cloak, the horse beside him stamping. *And the law?* Such simple words, easily said and answered, in syllables. Suddenly Rome lay clear about her, all those towering, columned buildings heavy not just with travertine and marble but with blood, spattered life, the long wrenchings of history. She saw those narrow, dark streets along which she'd hurried, all those watching eyes. And in that instant, in the bright sun, Xenia felt herself exactly as she was: a foreign young woman, unmarried, alone, with no people or parents or rights, imagining she could defy both Augustus and nature.

She looked at Ovid, sunlight dazzling her eyes, and thought that she saw something—she saw everything fall. A faint image, noiseless. But before it could clarify, his eyes fixed upon her with that *look*, that wordless exchange, and it was gold welding them together, ichor hot in her veins. He nodded.

Then she heard her instructions fly out to Persilla, as clear and light as a bird. She saw herself pass through the dark atrium that she had turned to a jungle, back into the light, onto the glaring granite road. Down toward the river, then the sharp bend back; she seemed to float beside herself and see her pale form moving. A seagull joined her, hovering above; the cypresses alongside seemed to shuffle and follow; the stones beneath her hurrying feet nearly uprooted themselves to urge her on. She was Alcestis ransoming her husband from death, Psyche breaking free of the underworld, Daedalus winging through the air. Moisture slicked her palms and the backs of her knees. Her huge belly wobbled, eyes white and wild, mantle concealing her glowing hair, as she flew down that granite road.

Then, far above—

She stopped and stared. Up in the dry blue sky, a white line was slowly being drawn. A long, straight line against the blue, and it was not a cloud, nothing seen before, nothing possible: a miracle. She trembled, squinting. And then a hesitant, ecstatic

quiver ran through her. Was the sky itself opening, showing her
that she would break that stern law?

But as she gazed up at that miraculous line, she realized
instead, with a blow that nearly felled her: *Ovid.*

It was Ovid, what Ovid did. He could transform matter into
words that float in air and are held on the breath, that are
etched into wax, drawn onto papyrus again and again so that
they could then slip through the eyes or the ears of others and
be absorbed and believed, enrapturing, and go on and on that
way, never diminishing in strength, not after centuries, millennia. Words that form an ephemeral world, hovering between
page and dreaming eyes, eternal.

She felt as if she were dissolving, sea foam.

For what Ovid made, she finally saw: what he made was the
quinta essentia.

Xenia stood there, terribly light. She put a hand to her face,
her eyes—everything was so bright. The world shimmered
about her, her legs felt sheer.

And there Persilla reached her, there on the granite road,
between the two famous hills, beneath a white line in the sky
that, drifting, slowly dissolved.

7

Ovid was shaking when he left, seconds after Xenia herself had flown from the house. His eyes were like a wild horse's as he hurried in the opposite direction, up the granite-puzzle path. *Witch, witch, witch!* The silly word that didn't begin to encompass what it meant kept hissing at his ears, almost the first word he'd ever said to her.

He felt again, from his teeth to his groin, a wave of rage at how she had denied him last night, how she had simply turned her head and kept what she knew inside her small mouth. Despite how he'd sobbed, despite how he'd begged. Spiteful, malicious! The thoughts came hot and furious as he hurried: she could not possibly love him; she'd simply made use of him and done all of this herself. Yes: first drawing him to her from the sea, and binding him with spells so that he'd carry her away; then constructing her own world about him, suspicions heaped upon her own greedy, foolish thoughts; now denying the one thing he asked. For he swore that last night he'd have thrown everything away. Yes, he'd have burned this nearly finished, marvelous project and scattered the ashes on the river, if she had only told him.

He shivered as he strode up the sunny hill, his feet heavy upon the gray stones. It was loathesome, what she was going to do tonight. Horrific. He'd seen that knife, that unfocused look in her eyes. And with the cat! Witch! She'd drag that boy's little empty body out somewhere. There would be a slicing, some hellish concoction, a hideous stirring of innards, cat's blood poured in. He'd heard about this kind of thing. There'd be steaming, smoking, a howling from somewhere. Just let the poor boy be dead!

Yet, here was just what he needed to launch the final scene. In another few weeks—afterward, that is, after the thing had been born—the moment would come. His hands sweated, just thinking about this, for he had never formulated it as he now did. The moment would come when he would have to dull his eyes like a shark's, draw her into the dining room, close the door gravely behind her, and say, sorrowfully, that she must go. Admit to her, when pressed, that he'd found his feelings had changed. Admit to her, when further pressed, that his feelings had more than just changed—he'd become, frankly, horrified. After what she had done with that dead little boy! Not to mention the *danger*, the tremendous risk to which she, doing such odious things in the open, had exposed him. It would be best if she was gone by morning.

Of course, he would go on, offhand, perhaps already leaving the room, already fingering the doorknob, *Of course, you will leave the child*. Or children—if she knew as much as she claimed. *They'll naturally stay with me*.

She'd stiffen at that; he'd see those white points of her teeth before she pressed her lips tightly together.

And who will care for them? she'd say after a time, all icy breath, that green tinge gleaming in her eyes.

Who will care for them? You needn't worry about that. They are—he'd say then, watchful, wary—*mine, after all, you know.*

The children. That's how the law works. Civil law, and natural law. You don't have anything to do with them. And so they won't need you any longer.

I see, she'd say coldly. *The law.*

Do quite understand, he'd have to go on, with a rattle of keys and equestrian authority, noting how she grew dangerous, *that you will certainly not take them with you.*

I do quite understand, she'd say, and her rage now would flame. And then she'd press on, insinuating: *But you haven't quite answered my question. And I can't help but be interested: who will care for them when I go? As a mother might, I mean.*

At that he'd have to sigh, and turn to her, and shake his head sadly. All his height would come into play, his angularity, his age, his disdainful nose. *Do you really imagine,* he'd say, weary of the dry, dull topic; *do you really still imagine that there is another woman? After all this time, is that what you actually think of me? No matter how I've changed, how I've sworn my honor.* He'd say it with just enough disappointment. *You've destroyed us, you know,* he'd go on. *Your spying, your constant suspicion. Did you think anyone could endure it? Very well,* he'd shrug. *Believe it, since you already do. Believe there is some other woman.*

Then, with just the right distant gaze of the eyes, just the right private tone, he'd add, *But yes, there is someone who will care for them. Who will take a—particular—interest.*

Out would come the tips of those talons. But she'd hide them; she'd remain icy cool; she might even just walk away. Then, however, she'd do it. Savage. Over there in her rooms, where they lay milkily dreaming. Rather than leave them to *him* and to this hated, invisible *her.*

A singsong, a low lullaby, and then . . .

Ovid stopped, his scalp sweating in the sun, his wrists practically dripping. He rubbed them against his sleeves.

Let's say she *tried* to do it, he went on, his eyes staring and white as he thought. *Tried*: he'd stick with that word, so *imperfect* in the true Latin sense, unfinished. Let's just say she went with that haughty back of hers to her rooms, and gathered the baby, or babies, or whatever there was, and then began to do what she'd do. Well, couldn't he stop her? He'd trail her, unseen. He was *bigger* than she was.

A hysterical giggle escaped him, there beneath the umbrella pines, halfway up the Palatine. Couldn't he just step in at the crucial point, overpower the maddened creature, pluck the little squirming packages, and—

He found that he could not go beyond that. Because what would *he* do with them? He, poisonous?

He shuddered away, his back pressed against a scaly pine in the shadows, looking out distractedly over Rome. He certainly wouldn't want them. How could he live with something like that? No one would want them. Give them away, to a slave? Sell them? Then why let them live at all, unwanted? Why not just let her do it, finish the wretched things off! It happened all the time! They were killed all the time! Exposed on hillsides!

Put out on the sea.

He felt himself breaking apart, glacially, his parts sliding away from each other. *Oh god*, he thought. *What am I doing? I am lost. I am lost in this monstrous contrivance.*

The sky seemed to whirl, bits of blinding blue spinning up beyond the pattern of boughs. He blinked, stubbed his toe hard against the tree's tough roots, ripped free a handful of needles, and pressed them to his nose. He stepped away from the pine and back onto the path, placed one long booted foot firmly upon it, and forcefully billowed his cloak.

To see, perhaps, his own shadow large upon the ground.

Somehow—although he swung about as always; although he stretched his neck and deepened his voice as he read and answered her questions; although he looked down the full length of his nose—Julia detected his delirium. It must have shown in his eyes. She coolly saw, and he *saw* her see, a crack forming in his chalky shell, a crack that, while she looked on and administered just a few clever taps, ran splintering and branching around him, until he broke.

And out it came. The whole evil thing.

When he looked up, emptied, from that puddle of filth, Julia was smiling.

"Yes," she said. "I know."

She'd known all about it all along. She'd seen her. And seen, very soon, what he planned.

"You weren't quite careful, were you?" she said, and laughed at his anguished face. "No, no," she cried, warm and consoling. "Really, I have excellent slaves. Absolutely invisible."

And, she said, the whole thing was brilliant.

"Besides," she went on, a smile barely contained in her mouth. "What makes you think the babies are unwanted?" She smiled now fully; she beamed. "They're not unwanted at all."

And, saying this, she placed her hands upon her lap. It was then that Ovid noticed that the pregnant globe at her middle was awry, that something about it was not right.

He realized then, too, what he'd long denied knowing: Augustus had no knowledge that Ovid was there, sponsored by his own granddaughter. This young woman acted alone, and acted entirely through hate.

8

Xenia stood for a long time at the hairpin turn in the granite-puzzle road, between the two famous hills. Long after Persilla had reached her, and spoken to her, and floated back to the house, she stood, her shadow clinging to her feet, her pale head high and alone in the air. All around was Rome's humming and smoke, but she heard and saw nothing.

What is it? she'd said, startled, as she felt Persilla's hands on her shoulders. *I have to hurry, there's no time!* She pulled away, but those tiny hands managed to hold her; the small, cloudy creature blocked her path.

It's illegal, Persilla said. The milky eyes looked into hers, and Xenia blinked and tried to pull away.

Persilla shook her head. *Don't you know what they'll do? They'll tie you in a sack full of rats and throw you into the Tiber. That's what they've done since Augustus. There are no more witches in Rome.*

Xenia stood there, squinting in the sun.

I know, she said helplessly. *But—he does it with me* was all she could say.

Persilla regarded her. *Does he.*

Xenia felt the sea open up black leagues beneath her, but Persilla went on.

Do you know what he does with you?

Writes, she said weakly.

But do you know what?

Xenia looked at those ancient gray eyes, and it seemed her clothes fell away; she was a naked thing, blind and foolish. After a moment the old woman let go of her arms.

The boy's already gone, she said.

Then she turned and went back up the path, and Xenia simply stood there, in the glaring light, at the hairpin turn in the road, the river glinting far behind her. There was that throb of Rome, the sun in her eyes, the heavy feeling of stone, of granite and marble and onyx and slate, like broken teeth in her mouth. She swayed, both feet on one irregular slab. She was floating; the ground was sea. The luminous line had faded.

After a time, she heard something. Clear as bells, the words said themselves in her mind:

White false hellebore. Mandrake. Nightshade.

Her head still high and wobbling, her shadow clinging to her feet, she turned and swam slowly over the stones, back toward Ovid's house.

9

After Ovid had gone, Julia sat still for a while, the world about her motionless. She traced a gold-sandaled toe over a spray of seaweed and heard the light, tinsely scrape. She laid both ringed hands upon the globe at her belly and briefly imagined—the imagining itself flitting in through the window, full of light and warmth—that what she touched was what she pretended, small and alive. For an instant she felt the whole swath of it, of love and tearing loss.

She opened her eyes again and let them roam over the walls, all illusory garden with fanning peacocks, striped snakes, diving swallows, rabbits with their gray ears up—all rosemary and sun, as if she were outside and free. Which she had never been. She had been born beneath eyes that, the second they'd bitterly discerned her sex, had already enslaved that soft apricot cleft to the requirements of Rome.

Sometimes it quivered through her so violently that she shuddered and felt she could open her mouth or poke fingers into her hated lower lips and pull it out, that hot snake of hatred.

Standing abruptly, she untied her sash and shook loose the hidden cushion. Ridiculous that anyone believed it. Yet they did. The court had been tender; her grandfather, beholding her, had slit his lashless eyes, and his skeleton hand had trembled as it touched her shoulder. But where he touched her she imagined a print of cold, that fragment of her flesh detached and swirling in the air of history, backward, becoming the piece of flesh bitten from Pelops's shoulder—Pelops, who had been served by his father for dinner, thereby launching a curse that would kill kings in their bathtubs, fell Troy.

Julia touched her shoulder. Kingdoms did fall. Troy, tragic Athens. She tried to imagine it, with her hands out at her silken sides. She tried to see this city of hers, this entire empire, razed into the earth. Shutting her eyes, she turned her body to the north, where as far as one could imagine everything belonged to Rome. Now she turned to the east, where the same was true; and to the south, the west. All the world belonged to Rome and fed it—not just the grain necessary to those million people down there but slaves, and silk, and hair in all colors, snipped from the heads of Gallic or Asian girls caught by Roman soldiers far off in the north or east. And the fine pressed powders in subtle silvery shades that came from somewhere up north, with which she was to shadow her eyes and lighten her forehead; and the deep red unguents for tinting her lips; and the saltwater eels that were always served grilled; and the tiny, tiny singing birds; and the pearls that someone, somewhere dived for; and the clusters of smoked fish eggs . . .

All these valuable goods that were painstakingly shipped through seas and rivers until they reached Rome, the center of the world; all the precious sculptures and countless blocks of cloven stone; all the thousands of marble columns, ribbed and ridged through sweating men's labor, crowned with acanthus and carved ram's horns: Julia tried to imagine all of it ruined. She tried to see the pediments with their reliefs and inscriptions falling, so that down would go the chiseled names of consuls and prefects and senators. She wanted the aqueducts to topple into valleys and upon the famous Roman roads, leaving heaps of pulverized brick. And that tremendous hieroglyphed needle, for which her grandfather had ordered an entire ship to be made, to haul it back from conquered Egypt—she wanted it to shiver as it shattered upon the ground. And oh, the millions of bodies beneath all this wreckage, reduced to what they were all along, masses of pulp and blood, senseless. Then, the world torn open, how the beasts, smelling the chaos and blood, would break free from their dens, come blinking out into the sudden harsh light!

Yet as Julia stood fiercely imagining in the middle of her painted room, she found that she saw nothing. She heard the words of ruin, she felt the terrible hunger for ruin, but she could see none of it. A blackness, a sparkle, that was all. Her fingernails were driving into her soft palms, and she held her hands out before her, saw the faint red crescents she'd made.

Suddenly she felt enormously tired. All she could do was make a few smarting incisions. She could barely lift her own legs or arms, barely move from the center of this strangling, jeweled room.

Oh god, oh Mother, she thought, covering her eyes. *What am I?*

But in that private darkness, the certainty returned. *What are you—you know what you are. The futile drops of semen, the seething drops of blood: Fury. That is all you are, all you need to be, small and made of nothing but your slim yet valued body, and your forgotten but monstrous head.*

She would not tell. No one would know. Not until the end, when her grandfather lay dying, once the hideous progeny were assured—then she would lean close, lovingly as always, and tell Augustus her secret. And pull just as lovingly away, eyes shining, hair tumbling loose, to watch him below her, on his death cushion, as his mouth tore open, dry and wordless, and his eyes scraped around for help, his old yellow nails digging into the mattress. Yes, just then, only then, would she slip in her worm.

When Ovid left Julia, he walked blindly to the baths. His boots struck the paving stones with an underwater clang, a slow reverberation. The cypresses shuddered slowly by, and the pines, and the shining leathered faces of men in the square. He went into the changing room, dropped his satchel, and only when its weight struck his foot did he look down at it, and acknowledge.

He shook his head. He could not think.

He walked naked into the great room, fell into the water, and sank into the silent, greenish world that was so warm and forgetful. He turned, enveloped, sinking, and let his body bump to the bottom. There he lingered, fingers scraping the floor, penis swaying, eyes lifeless and open; he imagined himself drifting there forever.

But slowly he rose; he could not help it. His body turned, lifted, and broke through the surface, into the loud air of the hall, the steam, the echoing of men's voices. He felt the warm water lapping at his ears, and knew that it was blood.

The feathers are gone, he thought. They've slid free from the melted wax, and you have fallen into the sea. Imagine being so foolish as to trust yourself, in empty air, to wax.

For a moment, floating, he saw Horace's feathered man: the poet transmogrified to eternal bird, sprouting plumage and wrinkled horny claws, fluttering up into the sky. *So long! Thanks! I won't be needing a tomb.*

Ah, Horace. *Horace* could make jokes. With that wizened head, those dolphin eyes—one look at him and you knew: this man would live forever. When Horace had read his sacred poems for Augustus, on that sacred day, Ovid had wanted so hard to think, He is an emperor's mouthpiece. But Horace's words themselves settled upon that thought and dissolved it. He would live forever; he was as genuine as earth. It could not be described, the value of his words. Like a secret kind of water that is heavier and colder than the usual kind, words had more value in his lines than they otherwise had; they were coin, far finer than coin. Ovid, that day, invisible among the crowd and disdained by the emperor as he deserved, had stood listening, with a garish grin.

He moved his jaw in the water and felt it creaking on its hinge. Like the cow his Daedalus made for Pasiphaë to hide in and receive the bull, he was grotesque, a contraption.

There had never been wings, just stuck-together stage wings. All contrivance, not art. The plucked, bloodied feathers lay about him on the water, and he floated among them, sea-worms inching into his ears.

Xenia reached the dark doors and entered the familiar jungle. White false hellebore . . . deadly nightshade . . . or would mandrake be the best? Mandrake with its man-shaped root— although she thought the chicken-skinned thing looked more like what hung from a man; one shaved away the flesh. There it was, growing by the impluvium, with its spinachlike leaves and frail iris blossoms. So useful for bringing on torpor, and flying. Yet the weather was good—the day bright, not cloudy—so hellebore was permissible, too. And the sleep it brought was deeper.

Young spring hellebore, fresh and vital! Xenia poked her hands into the soft, moist foliage and found it among the pots closest to the rectangle of rainwater. Its lovely leaves were striated, like a lily's. Wrapping her fingers around the leaves, she pulled, then shook the plant free of soil, went out to the garden and, at the fountain, tore off the hairy fibers, the leaves, and scrubbed the firm root clean. At her shadowy table inside she dried it; quickly, neatly, chopped it; spread it out in a pan; and slid it into the warm brazier.

She heard herself humming as she worked, her voice high and thin. But her trembling hands gave her away, as did that quavering sense inside her, like a warm salt sea that at each tilt of her head threatened to spill from her eyes. In her belly the twins lay terrified. One hour, two: the hellebore must be brittle. Then she ground it fine with her stone.

It was an oddly glittering day, all the colors and surfaces like wet glass. The sea wobbled inside her. She kept her head steady as she sat, the small vial of powder safe in her pocket, waiting until he came home.

10

Such a lovely evening! Ovid strode energetically through the garden toward Xenia. She had watched from her dark room as he stood in the study, his eyes fumbling toward her, blind. Then she'd seen him find her in the darkness, flinch, gather himself, and come out.

Truly spring now, isn't it? he said, his eyes bright, fingers trembling.

She agreed. Truly spring! She let him take her hand and escort her through the portico, over the cool blue marble. The oleander blossoms were just beginning to open, with their dizzy smell. The air itself was thin, electric. Dinner with the doors open? She agreed—how pleasant! Her face felt like bright, wet glass. Falernian, this evening, he asked, or Alban? He eyed her with a nervous smile. He was pale.

The meal glided in and out between them, he on his scrolled couch, she on hers. Scallops from Tarentum, roasted truffles, red lettuces in a caraway sauce, black olives, the driest cheese. All prepared by Persilla tonight, because of poor Drusa . . . And dessert? He thought there were dates stuffed with pepper, fried in Attic honey.

She yawned, and he looked up anxiously. Was she tired? But wasn't she off tonight to—? The words had a fine, sharp point.

Yes, of course, she said; but she must wait until midnight. Then she shifted on her couch and began to rise but smiled, touching her huge belly. Did he mind? Her mantle was just hanging on her door—it was spring, but still rather chilly.

Of course, of course! Eagerly he leapt off.

And with him gone, the powder was quickly sifted into his wine and, dissolving, sank.

The dates were finished but he sat on, mulling over his Falernian. She went to her room and assembled her things, knowing that he would be watching, until the pupils of his eyes spread, wet and glossy. So with large, theatrical motions in the lamplight she gathered her knife, her vials and packets, the pair of dough dolls. As she passed by the dining room on her way upstairs, she noted the gray hue of Ovid's cheeks, the way his eyes were drifting. Out of sight, she crouched in the stairway and counted, with her breaths, to two hundred. Then she crept back through the atrium, moved noiselessly around the portico, and saw him, one long arm hanging, a lifeless finger in a puddle of wine.

Then quickly, quietly, through the atrium, down the hall. The sea pounded inside her; it crashed at her ears. She held the lamp before her and crept, the yellow light jangling in the darkness and catching the wide eyes of a deer, a startled nymph, the running hoof of a satyr. Halfway down the hall she faltered. She stopped and rested her forehead upon the painted plaster, sobbing in childish gasps.

But you don't even know anything! a voice cried out. Nothing—not really. There's still hope!

She lifted her head, her eyes dull and heavy, and followed the flame down the hall. Her feet dragged over the floor, into the black-and-white room, so full of his salty scent. The only man she'd ever smelled, or touched, or tasted, or known. The man she had adored.

His satchel lay on the floor, its shadow hovering close. On his table waited the scrolls.

The oil lamp flickered. Over it she lightly singed her palm.

The babies whimpered inside, protesting.

She could, still, just not do it.

But then, as she looked on from an odd distance, the shadow of her hand alighted upon the first scroll. One slender finger slowly slid the purple ribbon to the top, and off; the scroll's white skin sighed open. She parted the curl gently with her fingertips and bent her head over the surface, her hair falling loose.

And she read. First the warm, startling dedication. *In gratitude, to Julia* . . . Her finger tapped a moment, construing. Then she watched as her finger skimmed along the smooth white sheet, until it had reached the play's famous name.

Isn't it something how the blood can run cold.

Medea.

11

Late at night, gulls flew in flocks high over Rome, sharp beaks
open, crying out. The cypresses stood in somber rows, their soft
bark breathing the night air. Bright flames danced from the
eyes of lanterns; fishes swam in the lightless Tiber; underground, a lion stirred.

In her room with its seabed floor on the Palatine, Julia
turned over in her sleep, long hair lying in gleaming snakes on
her pillow. She seemed to feel something. She didn't wake but
tensed, as if her body were falling, yet she wasn't falling: something seemed to have entered. She twitched, uncomfortable,
one hand at her eyes. There was a story of a woman being
entered by a snake while she slept; there were many stories like
that. Or was it a sinuous, muscular cat that had crept in, a cat to
wrap her legs around? In her sleep she stroked the air near her
belly, her lean, punished belly, and her narrow thighs. Her
hands were empty. There was no cat, no snake. But something
had entered somehow; had something come into her room?

She sat up suddenly, afraid, hair wet at her neck. A gull
shrieked; she heard her heart pound. In the dusty darkness of

her room there hung a faint, bluish glow. Julia stared at it, in terror, understanding without words that she was seen, and known, and judged.

After a moment the light dissolved. But she sat in her bed, still staring, sweating, and her hands fumbled to her belly.

Down the Palatine, in the house on the grassy cleft above the cloaca, moonlight grazed the pockmarked herm. Ovid lay on his scrolled couch, an arm dangling to the floor, one finger half dead in a puddle. He was underwater, his naked body rolling.

Now, in the darkness, someone entered: that long hand was lifted by another and placed upon a tense globe. Still his body turned on the lifeless seafloor; still he tumbled in the coldest depths. But as his palm touched her living stomach it grew warm, and there came to him, through all the inky, poisoned leagues, a wavering ray of light—as if, through his hand, he were given her vision. He felt his eyes open in terrible wonder, he felt his mouth open in a cry as he *saw*—but again he fell back, and under.

Rome at night was wild, unfamiliar, but Xenia glided through it like an eel. Torches flickered from stone masks; young men marched chanting in packs; all through the air was the groaning of wheels.

She hadn't, two or three hours ago, or whenever it had been, raged. She hadn't slapped her hands upon his walls until the skin broke and left smears of blood. The room about her had not roared and hissed, despite all those panthers and snakes; their hides and scales had not rustled and clinked; their eyes had not blinked open. Her mind hadn't gone black; it had not been filled with animal blood, with the hot liquid desire to punish.

It had, on the contrary, grown clear. Everything about her had—the world seemed wonderfully light. She felt she had shed something, her limbs becoming clean and new.

In the narrow streets men's eyes followed her; torches sputtered as she passed; even a gull cried out harshly, agitated, swooping low. But nothing touched her or came near. There was something cold about her, palling.

She was walking from the labyrinth of the city toward the river, with long steps, her dress and ghostly hair flying. The arched theater was behind her, and she could smell the spring vapors rising up from the Tiber. Her stomach wobbled; in the moonlight she caught sight of her shadow. Strange shadow! It could not really be her.

So: her sweet tiny twins, her baby boy, baby girl, with their pink nuzzling mouths and tickling fingers—she nearly laughed aloud, in the moonlight by the river, not to have known all along what they were. A little Ovid and Julia, plotting from the start. Even now they whispered—she heard them, she realized, pausing in her steps. They were still goading her, sharp silver spurs upon their baby-soft heels, fine pointing nails on their thin fingers, tearing and ripping her membranes inside. There were insects that did that, ate their way out.

She was standing then at the bend in the river, its brown skin snakily glinting. There were so many different ways to proceed! The very substances she'd just been pondering—mandrake, white false hellebore, nightshade. No little baby hearts could stand much of them. Wouldn't the devious things be surprised—she'd give it, lovingly, in milk. Then how their water-blue eyes would change, how their little clinging fingers would stiffen!

But no: she wasn't thinking. Again she walked, gliding, brisk, while beside her the river flowed. There were literary precedents to be followed: *he* would appreciate that. What would be the very best? She paused, considering, and nearly laughed with delight when it came to her. The best, she decided, walking once more, was the vengeance of Philomela, Ovid's own spectacular version: the girl who was turned into a nightingale once she'd been raped by her brother-in-law; once she screamed she'd reveal him; once, to silence her, he pulled out her tongue and quickly sliced it off. How the poor severed thing cried out still, inching bloodily toward her feet! But her revenge was perfect—the little roasted child! Her own darling nephew! That would be sublime, to serve *that* up to him. Xenia would take over the kitchen for the evening. And save the small twinned heads for last, their downy hair in damp baby curls, their tender chins plumped upon the plates.

She laughed to herself, her dress flying about her. By now she'd followed the river out in its bow and followed it sharply back in. To her right, the mausoleum of Augustus rose in the moonlight, patiently waiting for the man's marble bones. Upon it grew stately cypresses, their roots stretching into the underworld.

Suddenly she found that she faltered, troubled by her plan: it seemed she hadn't been thinking quite clearly. For of course she mustn't wait to be rid of the little things, wait until all the agony of squeezing them out. What—and give Ovid what he wanted? Certainly not! Standing between the river and the cypress-covered dome, she chortled into the night air and slapped her stomach like a pony. No, no, no; she hadn't been thinking clearly at all: of course she wouldn't wait. She'd get rid of them tomorrow. Now. Before they were in the air, before they'd had a chance to open their little wrinkled lids and fix their milky eyes upon her, cursing.

She certainly wouldn't give him *that*.

The climax itself! The very point! What he had been dying for! The only scene left unwritten, in all that cool white scroll.

Certainly she wouldn't give him that to drop among the plump collection already in his jar. Her own shed wings were there already. How they'd beaten against the glass.

She continued swiftly up the river. So—

For *them*:

There were infusions she could use, of lupines, ox bile, absinthium. Or a bath of linseed, wormwood, mallow ... She'd have to bleed herself, and bleed quite a lot. Or she could use a pellet of brimstone, wallflower, or myrrh ... And if even that failed, she'd take a long needle.

She'd feel it, certainly, an exquisite torture. And there'd be another reaction, too, a shrinking, a shocked contraction. Then, after the struggle and the dissolution, out they'd come, in pieces. Little parts as transparent as newts but still recognizable—a foot, with tender toes; an ear like a new rose leaf, unfurled; a pair of tiny pink fingers, with nails.

For *it*, and for *her*:

White dittany—perfect! *Dictamnus albus*, burning bush ... Each part of the plant has lemony glands, so vaporous they ignite in hot weather; the roots can catch fire from afar. She'd rub the heart-shaped leaves upon his scrolls, the juices soaking into all those crisscross fibers. And there the flammable stuff would wait, in secret, for the touch of an eager hand, or the glow of lamplight.

And then, to the emperor:

> *Dear Augustus, Honored Sir:*
> *Do you know just what sort of egg your grand-*
> *daughter's got under all that silk? Untie the purple*
> *ribbons and see!*

"Ovum" she'd write, of course, for egg. And underline the first two letters, to help him put together the fine degree to which Julia had betrayed him. Treason, she believed it was called. Conspiracy?

And, at last, to *him*—just one short note, in his very own words:

> *I gave you your life.*
> *Now you're wondering—will I take it, too?*

She looked about her, startled. Here were Rome's northern gates, the end of the Flaminian Road; she'd walked very far. It was a long way home, and so late. The moon was paling already.

She'd better hurry. Perhaps she'd fly.

12

Ovid woke the next day late and sodden, red-eyed in his red dining room. The sun was high, baking the garden; he squinted and shielded his eyes. In his mouth, down his furred throat, crept an evil taste. He shut his eyes and tried to abolish any knowledge of his mouth. He tried to abolish any knowledge at all. But the very whiff of the stale puddle by his supine hand rose up, sickening, informing.

He managed to drop one heavy ostrich foot to the floor, to heave the other leg over as well. He staggered upright. And lurched, nearly retching, from the reeling room, out among the glaring columns, over the shifting mosaic floor, through the atrium, down the corridor, to his room. It was cool there, dark; he swayed a moment, eyes adjusting, his feet upon the skeleton. Then two large ape hands fell upon his table, a foul-breathed, bristling face followed, eyes frantically looking—but no, it was all right. The scrolls were still neatly tied, exactly where they'd been.

What had she done, then? What was the point?

Had she done something? Why?

A cauldron seemed to churn and bubble in his stomach. He belched, greenish, and paled at the stench.

He waited a moment, until the table had stopped wavering and the walls had stopped their warping. He bent and concentrated upon his precious scrolls. With a cold, shaking finger he slid away each ribbon, let each roll spring open, and ran quickly to the end.

Yes, it was perfectly fine. All there.

But did he smell something? Not unpleasant . . . in fact, rather lemony . . . He sniffed—but the violence of the little gust that rushed through his nostrils and into the cave of his skull was too much. Again he quaked, a darkness shivered over his eyes, the bronze bowl was clanking hurriedly on the floor, and out heaved the evil steaming mess.

He shut his eyes and rested his brow on one long, smelly hand as the events of the previous day appeared before him in pieces. So he was as reviled by Augustus as he'd ever been, and all along Julia had been devising a plot of her own. God, the implications . . . He struggled to breathe, struggled to think. Were there any grounds to think *he* knew what she plotted? What did it have to do with him, anyway? He would say, if pressed, if questioned, if *tortured*, that, after the departure of that disreputable person from his household, he had merely thought that nothing would be more suitable than to give the abandoned babies to his patroness. As slaves . . . How was *he* to have known what she'd planned? How could he be blamed? His giving them away was a proper sign of gratitude, surely. That she intended to pass them off—that she intended, it horribly seemed, to present them as the very flesh and blood of the emperor—*them*, the illegitimate children of Ovid, most reviled, most debauched poet, and a foreign, witchy, barbaric oddity: how could he be expected to have known that?

In fact, he now saw, he didn't know it. Not really. Really, he'd only surmised. *Really*, he'd only seen her hands, and that distressingly off-center belly.

He shouldn't even have looked. He hadn't tried to. That had been one of his better scruples all along: not to look at her that way, as might have been expected.

Maybe, in fact, he hadn't quite seen it?

Maybe he'd imagined it?

What, *him*—imagine?

Yes.

"Persilla!" He must wash, he must rise, he must drink some water; he must gather himself, he must work.

But *conspiracy, treason*, were the words that applied. He felt them wrap tightly around him.

He staggered to his feet, sweat sliding down his neck and sides, and struggled into clothes. But as he stood there, bare feet on his skeleton, he suddenly saw, with a force that made him buckle, what he had been shown last night in the darkness. For he had been allowed to see, just once, as *she* did. The warmth in his hand had spread through his body, a brightness had reached his eyes and nearly blinded him like Tiresias. And then that vision, in the glowing light: those small faces, his own children, in terror. A melting heat that he had never imagined rushed through him, and he put out his hand as if to stop what he was doing, but he felt himself sunder, felt his heart rip apart, and he stood there, a tree struck by lightning, splitting down to its roots.

Away from him now, away from that black-and-white room with its dancing skeleton; through the atrium and its breathing green plants, which would grow and creep and reach up,

thirsty, through the narrow compluvium as the years went
wandering by and the tufa walls slowly crumbled around them;
through those tall, winged black doors, which would rot and
fall from their rusted hinges; and up the granite-puzzle path,
which would gradually be buried in soil and weeds; over the
shapely shadows of the umbrella pines; to where the dry blue
sky rubbed away each day a few more grains from the Palatine;
there Xenia stood—she was remarkably light! As a moth must
feel, surely, after that long, cramped, moist time netted in its
own sticky membranes. She stood at the top of the hill and felt
wonderfully clean.

From here, up high, she could see everything. Moments ago
there'd been a wild crashing of cymbals as the eunuchs had
streamed out of the temple behind her, the Great Mother's temple, scattering petals and coins. She could hear them still as they
flowed down the path, shaking spears and blowing shrill pipes,
but the sound grew fainter. Even the gulls were beneath her up
here, with their ancient cries and ancient wings, swooping.
Before her, the terra-cotta and marble city stretched, rolled,
sighed, continued its slow consumption of the world. And
beneath the city, beneath the granite slabs—she could just
make it out—was the hot unrest of all those African animals,
sickened, confused by their journey, the strange human flesh
they'd been forced to eat sweating rankly through their oily
furs and leathered hides. There they were, under all the feet
that slapped busily upon Augustus's polished paving stones,
beneath her, in the famous marble square.

From this breezy bright bluff overlooking the city, she could
hear the voices. All those million voices inside those many-
colored, many-textured heads. They rose up around her like a
swarm of insects, droning wants, reliving memories, calculating

figures, making lists. Among them were a few clear voices, solitary, poetic, little pipes of air.

But behind them, much stronger, came the clamor of the gods. All the competing, manufactured gods, shrilling and hissing with their pointed tongues, or forked tongues, or tongues of snakes, or parrots, or bulls, all the tongues humans had given them. She heard the voices of the older, official gods, worn and juiceless at this age, but still watching with yellowed, spiteful eyes. And, more urgently, the voices of the newer gods, with the smell of wild youth, virile and secretive and stealthy at night. A mixed breed, brought like grain and fish eggs and sea dye and salt from the farthest strands of Rome's great stretching net. On the way, they were mingled and mangled and made thereby more impervious, a richer strain. These gods had the heads of dogs, women's full breasts, sinewy arms, the claws of birds or great cats; they had braided dark beards or lank pale hair and cold, opalescent eyes. They had a taste for bull's blood; their rites were carried out in caves. More secretive than those dustier gods, they resided in the private parts of people, in their loins, behind their sweating knees. She heard the jangling of their demands, and she could feel the bristles in her hand as the bleating head was jerked up, as the trembling pink throat was sliced; she felt the running warm blood; she smelled the smoking hair. Those gods were so jealous. They shoved and jarred for attention, jostling each other for the chance to be known, to draw the most blood, to have it pouring in their names down the paved roads, clogging the dust to mud.

Somewhere, even now, a lamb was being led up the altar steps, a lamb chosen for its perfection and purity: even its delicate hooves, its knobby, skinny legs, were perfect. The eyes of those who had chosen it were loving—they valued it, enormously. And the lamb itself? It felt this love and shyly looked up at the eyes around it glowing with desire. It would not comprehend that desire had different depths. Gratified, it would get to its knees, it would gracefully lie before its lovers, it would never suspect the blow.

Xenia looked up into the burning sky, at the drifting clouds, then down again, at the city. She smelled the hot underground fur, heard the faint clash of the cymbals, saw the hurrying white forms. But as she gazed down, something began to happen to all that marble, all those stones. One corner of the great square started to crack. Fine, branching dark lines were drawn across the square; the shuffling figures seemed not to notice. But then a few paving stones at one end actually buckled; in the other corner, several heaved. The southern end of the square was thrown open, the triumphal arches lost their footing; they trembled; they swayed; slowly, they fell. What a noise rose up to her ears! It was happening all over—her eyes flew now, dilated, excited: a cracking, a shaking, a wrenching apart, a tumbling. Mighty carved columns slowly fell, arches collapsed, pediments and roofs shattered, the statues were smashed to dust, the thin marble cladding broke free.

She put a hand to her eyes, until the thunder of toppling stone died away. After a time, the marble and brick dust settled. She looked again: it was mostly gone, the great city, ground back to earth or buried. Just a few broken columns were left lying or poking out of the ground, leaving only the hint of a plan. It was peaceful. Grass grew over it all, light and silky, sheening in the breeze. She could just hear the pacing of soft, small paws.

———

Earlier, there had been a ripping inside her, an exquisite, dividing pain . . . So excruciating, but she hardly remembered it now.

Now it was over, and she was so clean! So light! The wind rushed through her glassy hair. It flicked at her dress, as it had flicked at the dark water around her on that cold black night long ago. Her basket swung from her arm, a comfort.

Her last sense of Rome, in departing, was a wisp of smoke drifting from the Palatine, and a faint, trailing cry.

EPILOGUE

Out the port of Ostia, south along the boot of land, past an island where a solitary princess paces, then between monstrous Scylla and Charybdis, across the Adriatic and the Ionic, through the worst storms, then over the Aegean and the Hellespont, up the bright Marmara, through the Bosporus, and out at last into the Black Sea—on the western coast, not far from where the Danubius empties out its silt, Ovid sits on a rock, writing. Has it been only a year since the soldiers came to his door?

It is nearly summer. And in the warm air—perhaps there's hope. He has come out to the rock that protrudes into the marsh, and begins again his letters.

The fine bones of his wrist crack slightly as he scratches at his tablet. Behind him, to the west, are the crumbling walls of Tomis, and, somewhere inside them, his house. The wind howled all winter, whistling through the thin walls, within which he hunched night after frigid night, picking at a block of frozen wine. The land around Tomis is swamp; beyond the swamp are barren plains; barbarians roam on horseback. It's the edge of the world here, the tissues of civilization strained to their thinnest.

But far beyond—and Ovid *will* look far beyond, for he must cast his mind over this bleak land, make it wheel wild and hopeful in the sky—far to the southwest, where the sun will settle in such warm glowing streaks, is Rome. It's the first direction his eyes seek when he wakes, before the deadly realization drowns him.

His Rome. The knowledge of the city that is beyond his sight, all golden and living and marble, pulls at his heart so sharply that he moves a hand to his chest.

But this hand should be busy, he corrects himself: it should be writing, endlessly writing those letters to Rome.

Please.

I'm sorry.

Because maybe Augustus will change his mind and let him come back again . . . It hasn't been ruled out, after all. He's been given reason to hope.

When Ovid thinks of that interview, so very unlike the one he'd craved, Augustus's face is not there, just light, and a terrible, quiet rage. Ovid can still smell the burning skin, still hear Julia's ecstatic screams, still feel his own palms blistering as he slapped like a crow at the scrolls, all that evil brilliance in flames.

He looks out to the lulling sea and waits for his heart to grow quiet. It's louder now than it used to be; he hears it, at night, in his ears.

Sometimes, in the endless, wordless days, he allows himself to ponder what he found so long ago, far across these very waters. He thinks of her marbled skin, and of how she rose heroic from that pool, and of her terrible, strange eyes.

He never saw her after that night with the wine. She, her belly, her basket—all gone. Every trace of Xenia herself, and of what he had made of her, all but those two mocking lines. It silences him still, her decision. That she preferred to disappear.

He puts a hand to his eyes.

And the babies?

He cannot think of them. Whenever the thought of them rises, that fissuring begins and he shakes, he must actually wrap his arms around himself to hold himself together. But still he sees those tiny pale forms, crying in terror in the darkness.

He bends again over his tablets, suddenly old. He must keep writing. For Augustus *might*, one day, let him come home, despite everything he's done.

Dear Augustus, Honored Sir...

After a time Ovid fixes his eyes on the sea and thinks, I'd like a sign. I want to know if I will end my life in this place. It is rare that the words come so bluntly to him; usually he rubs them away. But he is barer now, after just one year; he feels his bones edging toward the air.

Sea birds are swooping and shrieking overhead—one, it seems, in particular. He glances up: its wings came close that time, and he does not like the look of its beak. It soars off into the sky, and he shields his eyes and follows. Far now, just a speck, it swings in great looping circles, drawing *O*'s and *O*'s against the blue. On and on they go, those circles, graceful and languorous . . .

Suddenly, with an irrepressible surge of ego, of desire, of wild awful *need*, Ovid believes that the *O* is for him. Immaculate, principal, ovate letter! Yes, it is—it is a sign—showing that he shall be fixed in the sky as he so awfully longs to be: borne aloft, transfigured, forever.

So people still read me? he writes rapidly now, warm tears dropping upon his tablet.

But again he hears the whir of wings. It has come back, that bird. Squinting up, one hand protecting the square of black wax, he realizes that the bird looks like *her*. That webby white, pigeon-yellow, gray . . . And there's something in its voice and its unblinking eye. It swoops especially close this time, and he swears he feels—he *smells*—its wings. His heart stops at the sheer animal redolence. The spite.

If she had only told him.

A flicker moves across the sea's surface, a chill breeze from the north. At that moment he understands: he will never leave this place. He will never be allowed in Rome again, that golden bowl of life.

And outside of it there is nothing. No life, no intelligence, he is nothing. His tongue goes stiff in his dry mouth. He will die here, alone. Forgotten.

Suddenly he is hollow. But he does not even apply the word, does not even think the sentence, for words and sentences have fallen away. There is just this water, this rock, this everlasting sky.

Does anyone still read me?

There's never any answer.

Does anyone know who I was?

Now, around, around, on the other side of the Black Sea, Xenia is standing in the clear, rolling waves. Her coast is more pleasant than his, lusher, its topography more extravagant. She doesn't live quite where she did before, but to the south, where the coastline begins its westward curve. Not near the Phasians, but not quite out of reach, where the cliffs are sharp and black.

She thinks of Ovid often. Sometimes she finds herself knee-deep, her eyes fixed upon a spot in the west where water fuses into air, where she knows he sits, in his dim little house, all alone.

She sees how he has shrunk, how the olive skin on his so long, so loved, marble bones has pulled back. She sees the nightly scraping of his whitened, frightened eyes upon the bare walls of his shell. Sometimes, still, she has moments, when the sky is especially black, when the pain and fury surge in her throat, and she longs to fly over the sea and haunt him. But more often she just crosses her arms, tilts her head, and ponders.

Now and then, on particularly clear days, she thinks, Maybe I should just tell him what he wants to know. Send him word, folded up in a shell.

But she's never managed it yet. She's too busy.

It is the first day of summer, two years since that elegant Roman foot first crunched on the egglike black pebbles. The day is glorious, the sky like a great glowing bell. The sea is smooth and glossy; Xenia can see through it to her wavering yellow legs, her feet half buried in sand. Behind her, among the clumps of floating seaweed, a few cows idly graze.

She'll gather some seaweed this afternoon. *Phycos thalassion.* Make iodine from it for little cuts, and bloodred, waterproof pigment.

A swell rises before her and rolls around her hips. It's exciting every time, to feel that lift that has traveled miles; the cool wave passing by seems to carry her heart with it. Behind her the water lazily breaks, the pebbles clatter, and again the sea pulls itself in. Now another swell is forming, glassy green and smooth; it rolls toward her, slowly, thrilling—a surge of sheer physical delight rushes through her, and she cannot help but squeeze.

For clasped in each arm is a plump little body. Two pairs of marble-smooth, fat, kicking legs; four sets of dabbling pink toes; and twenty tiny fingers—which, at this moment, as the swell rolls forward, all reach toward the lifting water, trying to grasp an apricot jingle shell, which slowly, wobbling, sinks.

ACKNOWLEDGMENTS

I am deeply grateful to Becky Saletan and Geri Thoma for their clarity and care in helping me see my way through this book. For all their love and support—from my first reading of Ovid to the last checking of facts—I thank my family, as well as Rosalind Murphy, for teaching me Latin, and Tom Zigal, for first encouraging my work. Most of all, for bruises acquired on the Palatine and for providing the life, my love and thanks to Alex Wall.

Among the secondary sources that were most helpful to me in constructing a world around Ovid and Xenia were Peter Green's editions of Ovid's poems, with their excellent introductions and notes; Neal Ascherson's *Black Sea*; David Braund's *Georgia in Antiquity*; Richard Brilliant's *Roman Art from the Republic to Constantine*; Lionel Casson's *Travel in the Ancient World*; E. R. Dodds's "Supernormal Phenomena in Classical Antiquity"; Mary B. Lefkowitz and Maureen B. Fant's *Women's Life in Greece and Rome*; Georg Luck's *Arcana Mundi: Magic and the Occult in the Greek and Roman Worlds*; John E. Stambaugh's *The Ancient Roman City*; as well as Lesley Bremness's

Herbs. Physical sources include excavations at Pompeii, Herculaneum, Ostia, and Rome; the Archaeological Museum of Naples; the Museum of Roman Civilization; and the Palatine Museum. Among primary sources were works of Catullus, Horace, Juvenal, Pliny, Propertius, Quintilian, Strabo, Suetonius, Tibullus, Vergil—and, of course, Ovid.

Those who know Ovid will see that I have altered parts of his own account in forming this fiction—one in which I hope he might nevertheless have seen himself, if somewhat transfigured.